TENDERLOIN

ALSO BY JOY SORMAN

Life Sciences
À la folie
La peau de l'ours
Du bruit
Boys, boys, boys

JOY SORMAN

TENDERLOIN

Translated from the French by
Lara Vergnaud

RESTLESS BOOKS
NEW YORK • AMHERST

Copyright © 2012 Joy Sorman
Translation copyright © 2024 Lara Vergnaud

First published as *Comme une bête* by Éditions Gallimard, Paris, 2012

First Restless Books paperback edition April 2024

Paperback ISBN: 9781632063618
Library of Congress Control Number: 2023945832

Cet ouvrage a bénéficié du soutien du Programme d'aide à la publication de l'Institut français.

This book is made possible by the New York State Council on the Arts with the support of the Office of the Governor and the New York State Legislature.

This book is supported in part by an award from the National Endowment for the Arts.

Cover design by Jamie Keenan
Set in Garibaldi by Tetragon, London

Printed in the United States

1 3 5 7 9 10 8 6 4 2

RESTLESS BOOKS
NEW YORK · AMHERST
www.restlessbooks.org

The simplest way to identify with another being is still to eat it.

CLAUDE LÉVI-STRAUSS

TENDERLOIN

He's in the opening shot, swathed in white and dignity, wielding a knife. At first you can only see his chest bisected by an apron, and his hands gloved in metal. Then the camera pulls back, the young man appears in his entirety, all parts accounted for, from head to toe: a butcher.

The video speeds up, images streaming rapidly to an electro soundtrack with muffled bass: the butcher chops up hogs in fast-forward, disjoints vertebrae bone by bone, extracts a rack of ribs, carves a rump steak, scrapes fat from muscle, thrashes the meat with a hammer then a tenderizer, deveins livers and kidneys, grabs a nice-looking calf's head by the nostrils, removes the brain, unrolls some trussing string, tosses the meat onto a sheet of kraft paper, weighs it, and hands the packet to the customer.

You're not sure you caught everything. A thousand movements broken down into 152 seconds. Huge hands scuttling before the camera lens, palpating scarlet, gleaming matter beneath the projector lights. End credits, image frozen on the butcher's youthful smile: his eyes sparkle, radiant, his eyes are wet, it looks like the butcher's going to cry.

Pim is the star of a promo video for jobs in the meat industry, a simple amateur film that will be shown in the dining hall right before the welcome reception.

Two years earlier, young Pim is beginning his apprenticeship at the vocational center in Ploufragan. It's September, a cold wind is swirling above the trees in the small courtyard, the first autumn leaves flying low to the ground. The aspiring butchers gathered beneath the awning have turned their pockmarked faces toward the dais: the director is holding court, his voice carries, thunders in a solemn drum roll, *Gentlemen, young lady, welcome!*—he directs a smile both complicit and apologetic at the sole girl in the group. The director is three years away from retirement and old-school (like tripe *à l'ancienne*, a classic recipe—simmer in a marmite for five hours before dousing the meat with a glassful of pastis in the final hour of cooking—far superior to Caen-style tripe), shoulders forward, belly protruding, hands crossed behind his back, buckled shoes and charcoal gray suit:

Gentlemen, young lady, the first thing, which might seem like a detail but it's not: a butcher wears his hair short. It's a question of hygiene, of presentation. I see a certain number of you who will require a visit to the barber. Short hair is neater, it's easier, more respectful, too. As for you, young lady, you can get away with pulling yours back.

For some time already, tiny Technicolor images of short-haired apprentice butchers have been infiltrating Pim's slumber. They flash by like a slideshow or a sticker album, bright, persistent images surfacing from his REM sleep: sparse beards on their chins, these butchers have taken up permanent residency in the young man's transparent dreams. Visions of apprentices with crew cuts trimmed high on their necks, with reddened hands, with fingernails clipped at right angles and hemmed in by chewed pockets of skin, with socks pulled up tight. They smoke in secret and the smell of cold tobacco on their fingers mixes with that of blood, sharp and metallic, neither scent able to mask the other. In Pim's dreams smells are tenacious, they don't fade until a few minutes after waking, once his fingers curl around a cup of coffee.

Pim didn't always dream of being a butcher, it's not a calling, it's not taking over the family business (his parents are municipal employees, their dynamic the cool politeness of those who have never known the passion of discord and reconciliation), it's getting away from school (which at first left him indifferent, then bored him, and now ossifies him), it's finding a job, making money, get cracking as soon as possible, finding a trade and let's be done with it. Pim never feigned the slightest interest in pursuing the life of an intellectual, an academic career, on the grounds that a higher education would ensure he earned a decent salary, be given responsibility, attain a certain form of social merit. A diploma doesn't guarantee anything anymore, and certainly not lucrative and stable employment.

What's more, Pim is good with his hands, long, pale hands—more like a pianist than a butcher, his father always tells him—with slender, bony, and agile fingers. Pim has never broken anything, not even as a child; his movements are rapid and precise, and his fingers, despite their peculiar thinness, are full of life. He can undo the tightest of knots, untangle the thinnest of threads, steadily glue minuscule fragments of porcelain to a chipped vase, open beer bottles with his hands, make coins and rubber bands dance between his fingers, jimmy jammed padlocks.

The rest of his body is in the same vein: elongated, knobby, but acrobatic.

At an age when kids like beer, skateboarding, or rock, Pim likes his hands, they're his claim to fame in a way, he finds them efficient and elegant. For touching girls as well.

Pim looks at his hands and he cries.

Pim cries often, without cause and even without wanting to, the tears rain down out of the blue, inappropriate for the situation, unexpected and unjustified. His parents have stopped worrying about it or even reacting, it's been happening since Pim was little, and at school he was teased a lot. In the beginning they thought it was a tear duct disease, a syndrome of ocular dryness, like grains of sand in the eyes, needle pricks or burning, but no, the tears always come when they're not expected, at the wrong time, like a nosebleed that happens for no apparent reason. Pim cries at the sight of his hands or a dog crossing the street, at a chicken in the oven, at frizzy hair, and who can say if it's his emotions. He also cries when he's overwhelmed, unhappy, or angry and they're the same tears, the same salt, they deform the same long, angular face, hollowed beneath his bronze-colored cat eyes.

Pim observes his hands laid flat on his desk, his heart doesn't tighten, there's no lump in his throat, no churning in his gut, his legs are still supporting him, and yet he's crying. Absence of feeling, no sign of trembling, rather: water dripping from a poorly shut faucet, a leak in the line, a mechanical fountain.

He doesn't know it yet, but these hands will ensure him a bright future.

Pim doesn't understand economic mechanisms, market forces, or financial fluctuations himself, but still he pays no heed to those who profess the end of the artisan, judging such trades obsolete, doomed to extinction, the unworthy remnants of a long-gone stage of the economy. He happily leaves modernity's ghostly professions—marketing or communications—to others, will choose a dirty and concrete line of work.

Pim went largely unnoticed until the end of ninth grade, a mediocre student but polite, reserved, no drama. Halfway through spring semester, the guidance counselor hands him a brochure about apprenticeships—*Pim, these aren't dead-end jobs you know, this will guarantee you a good career*—but Pim isn't on the fence. The brochure promises training plus on-the-job experience, a vocational certificate in two years, over 4,000 positions to be filled across all of France's butcher shops, an apprentice salary ranging from 25% to 78% of the minimum wage, and a sector that's recession-proof. And why not baking, masonry, or carpentry? Because butchery is lucrative, because a butcher doesn't work outside in the wind and rain, and because meat motivates him more than wood, that's just the way it is.

This morning, in the school courtyard, they aren't much to look at: thirty teenagers with skin reddened by the wet sea wind, panic-stricken with hormones, budding fuzz above their upper lips, bangs plastered to foreheads, round cheeks, hunched shoulders, hands in pockets, slight in their jackets, buried in their hoodies, they crush invisible cigarette butts with the tips of their sneakers as they listen to the director deliver his pompous speech in a monotone. Pim, sixteen, is taller than the others by a head, his hair buzzed short, his gaze wide.

Two stand out immediately in this small gathering: Pim and the girl in the pencil skirt and riding boots. She's standing squarely, legs slightly apart, an aspiring butcher who won't settle for working the cash register and offering customers cooking advice and opinions on the weather, but who intends to wear the chain mail apron and wield the ham chisel. The director turns to address her as much as the others:

Nowadays women can become butchers just like men. The days of slinging carcasses over our backs are long gone . . . That said, to do this job, it's increasingly important to have a perfect understanding of animal morphology and food hygiene regulations.

They listen patiently but they already know all this, they read it in the brochure: "Butchery is an honored career path that encompasses a variety of activities, and diverse and overlapping skill sets and responsibilities."

You might find work as an artisan butcher, in a shop or working the marchés, or you could get hired at a cutting and processing plant that services restaurants, or maybe by a super-market chain.

They know, they read it.

What qualities are required to become a butcher?

11

They're holding their breath.

Like I said earlier, the first thing is good hygiene, that's non-negotiable. Next: manual dexterity, a sense of initiative, ease with the customers, and of course an aptitude for business. A strong work ethic and team spirit are equally indispensable and I would also add an appreciation for a job well done.

Pim is on edge, the wind is spinning in tiny gusts, he glances at the chestnut trees already covered by yellowing leaves—this year the parasite-ravaged foliage is tipping prematurely into autumn.

As you no doubt already know, you will have one week of classroom instruction every three weeks. The rest of the time you'll be doing actual butchery . . . a sector unaffected by unemployment . . . you must always prepare your meat as if it was for a member of your family, with the same care and the same love . . . a starting employee earns 1,500 euros per month, before taxes, an experienced butcher between 3,000 and 6,000 euros per month . . . the average Frenchman eats 200 pounds of meat per year . . . in "artisan butcher," the most important word is artisan . . . meat goes with wine . . . historically, butcher storefronts were painted blood red . . .

The apprentices are restless, a slight rumble swells like a blanket of fog, spreads throughout the courtyard, a rumble composed of mumbling and cleared throats.

. . . so welcome everyone and let's honor this beautiful profession.

The students applaud at last, halfheartedly, then scatter only to immediately gather in small confabs by instinctual affinities. Pim is going to grab a smoke on the sidewalk, his last one. He's decided to quit, the taste of Royal menthol marrying rather badly with the smell of meat, the green packet clashing with the red flesh. He's decided to quit at the risk of disappointing the girls so fond of his mentholated kisses, vigorous tug-of-wars that leave a delicious tingle, an electric shiver on the tongue and gums. His kisses will no longer have the peppery taste of cigarettes but the girls will win in the long run since Pim plans on renting a studio downtown with his apprentice salary.

Pim has two years ahead of him to learn to be a butcher, the tools, the gestures, and the techniques. Two years isn't much to master bookkeeping, labor laws, animal anatomy, European standards, the cold chain, certifications and labels, protected designations of origin, product traceability, presentation, decoration, and labeling techniques, to learn how to dress poultry and prepare tripe products. In two years, Pim will receive a vocational training certificate and the status of qualified butcher; he can then obtain his professional license, specializing in pork butchery, in order to stack all the odds in his favor.

This kid doesn't have the build for the job, thinks the carcass processing instructor when Pim walks into the first class of the year. That kind of skinny won't do much to reassure the customers, it's not exactly inviting, being greeted by a body stretched out like a long vein. An all-steak diet would do him good, while we're at it let's give him the cow's heart so his pale skin flushes red, so the steer can transfer its power, have him gulp down some blood pudding, eat the *boudin* rare, raw even, until his arterial flow pumps stronger, serve him *steak-frites* with half a bottle of red, you're thirsty huh Pim, here, hand over your glass, this will toughen you right up.

Need to fatten up, son. You eat meat at least? Yes, sir, of course, it's genetic you know, I eat for four but nothing helps. So you're a jittery kid then. No, sir, I'm very calm, you'll see.

And the apprentice butchers certainly do seem gentle, gentle and melancholy against a backdrop of white earthenware and fluorescent lighting, in their knee-length coats and in the cold, a cold that is only just beginning—the cold of the back room where meat is prepared, the cold of the cold room, the cold of the outdoor butcher stand, the cold of the slaughterhouses and wholesalers at dawn, they appear tender and clumsy before their sharp tools.

Pim, stop staring at the knife like a dumbass, pick it up and start carving. If you want to learn how to cut you don't admire

14

the knife, you use it, just like everything else. Do you know why humans are more intelligent than animals? Or, as they say, at the top of the pecking order? 'Cause we have hands. You ever see a hen with hands? Or a cow? Yeah, didn't think so.

The very first week of the program, Pim is hired as an apprentice at the Morel butcher shop in Ploufragan where he shows up for his interview wearing an immaculate white shirt slightly puffed over a concave chest that can never quite fill out articles of clothing, and new, ironed jeans, and black full-grain leather moccasins. The proprietor (Morel himself)—an enthusiastic man in his fifties afflicted with permanent rosacea acquired from the blizzard of the walk-in fridges—shakes Pim's hand vigorously and at length, leaving the scent of chlorine and freshly ground meat on the apprentice's palm. He insists on the importance of transmission in the field, on the courtesy sometimes lacking in the younger generation, adds that you need to be passionate to do this job, to prepare beautiful products, to get out of bed in the middle of the night and spend hours in the cold room.

But Pim isn't afraid of anything, not fatigue or the cold or hard work, he's only scared he'll suddenly burst into tears for no reason in front of the boss as he trusses a chicken and get himself fired for excess sensitivity or poor hygiene—crying into the sausage meat isn't ideal.

He isn't afraid of anything, and he's in a hurry. To make it, to earn money, to live his life. That's why he assures Morel that he's willing to carry out all the thankless tasks, starting with cleaning the prep area—finishing the scrubbing every night after the others are long gone. He knows he'll feel at home in the back room where terrines and sliced meats are prepared, the beginner's block on which he'll practice the majestic art of carving and where the shit is washed away. Pim isn't proud, Pim is sensible and focused on his goals: become a butcher, identify the different parts of the cow, and wield the blade.

From the first hour of the first day he dives headfirst into butchery, like a zealot, a diehard chained to his vocation, to his immediate and all-encompassing addiction.

And we'll see how Pim will go mad for meat.

His first day at Morel's butcher shop, Pim clocks in at 6:00 a.m. and clocks out at 8:00 p.m. He starts by cleaning the prep room then devotes the rest of the morning to observing; he watches the other butchers carve carcasses, remove bones, discard superfluous skin and fat. Silently standing to the side, in his white coat, hands behind his back, Pim notes the choreography being performed before his eyes, all the while tensed for possible tears that will not come.

The second day, still observing, he switches to the shop side, the customers peeking into a glass window jam-packed with galantines, impeccably larded meat, chicken with feet gloved in white paper sleeves, and escalopes dozing on lace and parsley-side. Behind the counter, the butcher plays his part beneath a small framed poster, *French Lamb: A Cut Above!*, shows off his expertise on the block, mincer dancing, *bam* some tender muscle slapped onto the cutting board, *still a little left should I wrap it up for you?* roast veal barded and trussed in a dazzling performance, meat gently tossed onto the scale, wrapped, weighed, *who's next*—the theatrical performance of a job well done.

On the third day Pim arranges the animal carcasses in the cold room, cleans the fridge where the andouillettes are kept, peels carrots to spruce up the terrines and pâtés. The days go by, the apprentice works hard, he learns quickly, pig carving at 7:00 a.m. and mopping at 9:00 p.m. Mondays are for breaded pig's feet, Tuesdays *pâté de tête* (cook the pig head; when tender, debone and cut into cubes), on Wednesdays they melt lard and salvage the fat around the intestines to make tallow, Thursdays mean sausages (slide the large intestine onto the cannula, add the meat to the stuffer and turn), Fridays it's roast larding, and on Saturdays Pim is tasked with preparing ground meat, his favorite job. He gathers the driest pieces from above the ribs to crush in the machine.

Then, paralyzed by the beauty, Pim contemplates the mottled pink and white meat that emerges from the grinder like an invasion of maggots.

For the first two months the nausea is constant, stagnant and gnawing, verging on melancholic: the blood, the smells, the entrails, and the Clorox, but also the fatigue, the early mornings, the cup of bitter coffee drunk alone at the kitchen table, the stomach incapable of ingesting any food even as the body demands more rest. It's dark when Pim is the first to arrive at the butcher shop, the blinding fluorescent lights boring into his retinas, the cold of the stainless steel, the meat, the metallic apron and gloves a punch to the gut. It's still dark when the apprentice buries his carving knife in the meat and drops of blood fall silently onto the sawdust blanketing the tile floor.

Pim is rapidly gaining in dexterity and confidence but his movements are pained, his right arm constantly sore, his legs keep falling asleep from standing in one spot, bent over the worktable, his white skin is mottled with red, blood rushes and throbs in his stiff hand forever extended by a blade.

Yet week after week Pim repeats the same maneuvers and this repetition eventually cancels out the fatigue, numbs the pain, creates habits that take over his body like simultaneous waves of lethargy and adrenaline, torpor and ardor. By repeating his gestures he masters and understands them, he identifies his emotions. Just look at his beaming face—his wide-set eyes open even wider, sunken features swelling along his cheekbones, he takes fresh pleasure in carefully separating meat from bone: not a single bit remains, the meat is perfect, clear and clean, no knife slashes in the fibers, no trace left behind, just a veil of red silk.

Everything delights him, just look at that face concentrating on the preparation of cured ham. Pim slowly rolls up his coat sleeves, sits his lanky body on a milking stool, knees splayed, steadies a bucket filled with coarse salt between his safety shoes, plunges the hams inside then rubs them vigorously in the direction of the fiber. The salt irritates the skin on his too-slender fingers, the apprentice cries warm acidic tears, but it's just the salt scattered in minute particles landing on his eyelashes.

Day after day Pim rubs without complaints, and as he rubs is already imagining himself artisan of the year, the blue ribbon in tripe-making, world champion in carcass-carving, the butcher's entire body of work, his legacy; Pim imagines himself a knight in shining meat.

One night, there's an argument between another apprentice at the vocational school and Pim, who stands accused of having prepared ground meat in advance when as everyone knows ground beef is always made to order, in front of the customer. Pim contests—slander!—but the other apprentice stands by his version of events.

Pim suggests a duel, to settle the dispute and clear his name: they'll face off in a secluded clearing in Brocéliande forest.

On the appointed day, two butcher blocks are set up across from one another, fifteen feet apart. At sunrise, despite the opaque fog and freezing rain, the face-off begins. The apprentices take their positions behind the blocks labeled with their butcher shops' seals, slicing knives in hand, cleavers at their waists, aprons starched. Mr. Morel is refereeing the duel. Pim and his rival grandiosely sharpen their blades without taking their eyes off one another, they dry their palms on their coarse cotton aprons, they cross swords. At the sound of the horn, they each grab a hindquarter of beef, cleavers strike the wood with a crisp thud, and victory will go to whoever does the most beautiful job, the most beautiful carving. Now their fingers are tearing fibers from the meat, ripping off fat and nerves, gripping their knife handles, digging into flesh, massaging it, feverishly kneading. At the end of the prescribed time, Pim, covered in sweat, eyes sunken and ringed by a mauve veil, apron soiled, hands aching and trembling, is declared the winner.

The months pass and Pim doesn't miss a day, he always gives one hundred percent, always applies himself; he's even-tempered, precise, and meticulous, to the point that all his longings are eroded, absorbed by the meat, by the time the meat requires—no more friends, no more girls, no more free time, in a few weeks his life has completely changed, he wanted it to. Pim, already a solitary and reserved young man, is every day further engulfed by butchery, this craft that comes so easily to him and at which he excels.

Morel is proud of his apprentice, the sort of unfounded pride you might have for someone other than yourself. One night after closing he signals to Pim to stay, offers him a chair and a few slices of andouillette, pours him a drink and dramatically places his large hand on the boy's bony shoulder: *You're the best . . . you'll go far because you respect the job. You should know that the butcher is like a doctor, he has power, he holds his customers' lives in his hands. Don't ever forget that. You can die from eating bad beef, if the meat's gone off, if it was poorly prepared, if the cold chain is broken. There are pieces not even a dog will take. You have to know how to conserve the meat, you can age it for a long time, as long as you keep the fat on the carcass.* But once the blade pierces the meat everything happens very quickly, you carve a pathway for bacteria and the once-protected muscles ripen, then go stale, spoil, the meat sits forgotten in the back of the fridge. Red turns to shimmering brown, to green, the smell of ammonia and sewer drains is nauseating; the meat is now poison.

This was the day Pim realized he could kill a man with a spoiled skirt steak, a thought that induced great anxiety, anguish really, and oddly enough, his sex drive returning with a vengeance, it made him want to sleep with a girl. He thought about the girls he had been neglecting for months.

But are girls attracted to butchers? Do girls want to sleep with boys who smell of Montbéliard sausages, braised meat, herb-roasted chicken, and coagulated blood? Because the smells linger on the butchers, on their clothes but not only, the smells embed themselves in the fibers of their hair, beneath their fingernails, seep into their skin, and their entire bodies reek. It's no good washing, scrubbing, it stays. Pim would have needed two weeks of vacation, far from Morel's butcher shop, in order for the smell to completely disappear. It's there all the time, heady and familiar. Pim doesn't notice it anymore, sometimes wears cologne to mask it, when there's a family dinner. A smell of rawness and freshness, of leaded blood and detergent, that penetrates his protective rubber gloves and abrades his skin. Are there girls for whom this smell of wood and hard labor elicits an *I love you* in the back of the throat, an *I love you I'm going to eat you? Pim, did you hide raw veal kidneys in your boxers? If the juice ran down your thighs I would lick it.*

Before, girls used to like Pim for his gentle cat eyes, because he radiated kindness, for his body sharp as a bill-hook and his mentholated kisses. And because he took his time, patience rare in a sixteen-year-old boy, and shared his cigarettes, because he didn't say much but would affably watch from the sidelines. Before, Pim used to meet girls at school or at the square on Saturday nights when everyone hung out on the benches well past midnight. He hasn't been back to the square in months. Tonight the air is tender and the light fading, it might be a good time to stop by, to meet a girl and invite her to come sleep on the sofa bed in his IKEA-furnished studio.

In the small square filled with chestnut trees, fifteen teenagers are milling around benches, packs of beer, rolling tobacco, propped-up scooters, couples intertwined, girls sitting on boys' knees and vice versa. Passing iPod headphones from ear to ear, like divers sharing a mouthpiece, they exchange hip-hop songs, commenting at length about this historic sample or that bass line which they play on cell phones transformed into loudspeakers, and the night deepens, they shiver, open bottles with their lighters, devour bags of barbecue-flavored chips, lick their fingers and laugh.

Pim is welcomed with exclamations, pats on the back, and pecks from girls standing on their tiptoes so they can reach his cheek, at the summit of his six feet two inches. *It's been ages Pim, you work too much.*

Yet many of them are also apprentices (baking, plumbing, or hairdressing), others scrape by on odd jobs, some are still in high school or exiled to Saint-Brieuc during the week for vocational studies or a first year of community college. Everyone dreams of getting out, of leaving Ploufragan and its eleven thousand inhabitants, its gusts of wind laden with salt water and capable of penetrating a light jacket, of leaving behind the gray stone, the group of deadbeat friends hanging around the neo-Gothic church, the blinding green of the Goëlo valley, of abandoning the megaliths, the shaded undergrowth, the reservoir around which summer days drag on, flat, of leaving this industrialized countryside they don't see a way out of. Or else get a job at the Zoopole, major in science, buy a suit downtown, and end up at the Institute of Research on Livestock, Health, and Hygiene, or the Center for Porcine Pathology. Otherwise, really, leave.

Pim is thinking seriously about it: open a butcher shop in Paris, the city with the best butchers in the world.

With a single jerk, he opens a Budweiser against the edge of the bench and tears rise in his eyes as the head rises into the bottleneck. His lower lids are instantly rimmed with salty liquid as the hop foam surges up then slowly escapes, sliding down the bottle. Everything's overflowing. Pim dries his tears on the back of his sleeve, licks the rim, the others don't stop their conversation, make like they didn't see anything, they know that Pim cries, that he's been crying since forever for no reason. *Pim are you sad? No. Are you in pain? No. Are you feeling emotional? No way. But Pim you're crying. Yeah, looks like it. Hey, who shook these beer bottles huh? Not cool.*

Pim, you're worse than a chick, and a stream of laughter laced with tobacco echoes loudly, amplified by the empty night.

On the opposite bench three girls are drinking white wine from the bottle, seated cross-legged apart from the group, they're talking in hushed voices, the domineering stepmother, the drama queen of a little sister, the ex without a backbone, the creepy teacher, unforgettable parties, secrets among girls, friends, the night. There's one Pim likes, her short hair, her small breasts, her tight jeans and Keds worn like slippers, they're sliding off, exposing tiny feet with chipped red nail polish.

Pim comes closer, *Hey girls mind if I sit down? Can't you see we're trying to have a conversation here? No one invited you. K, well, I'm Pim, I'm a butcher, and soon with a little luck I'll have my own shop, it's me who'll be selling you your Sunday roast and a slice of ham for the little one, when you're actual grown women. Go on, get out of here. If you need me I'll be over there on the bench, I'll wait.*

Pim walks away backward, his feline eyes riveted on the girl in the Keds, the girl with the defiant chin who holds his yellow, wide-eyed gaze.

Later that night she'll go over to Pim's bench. He's stretched out, hands crossed behind his head, long legs bent, the square is nearly deserted now, the remaining teens half-asleep beside their bikes, drunk on alcohol, weed, and conversation. Pim waited for the girl without really expecting her, she puts out her hand, *C'mon get up, I could go for a burger*, he grabs it, it's warm, so much warmer than the night air.

She's thinking about it of course. Thinking that she's going to sleep with a guy who carves meat all day long, impossible not to think about it, not to wonder what that's like. Hemoglobin-reddened hands that will go from a carcass to her breasts, jump from one kind of meat to another, expert, useful hands, hands that understand anatomy and can assess what they're holding, hands impossible to deceive, hands that handle the dead and tonight, finally, a living, dancing body.

But a completely naked butcher requires trust. She takes her clothes off first, he undresses with his back turned, she discovers a tattoo occupying the entire surface of his right shoulder blade, a prime rib rendered in deep and realistic vermilion. The perfectly curved image, embedded in the skin, rises to the surface like a membrane of blood. She comes closer, pinches, licks, nibbles the colored flesh, so thin in this spot, bites the skin, bold meat *jus* drips from the drawing, the shape of the tattoo adapts to Pim's body as it begins to move, the prime rib quivers and unfurls. She's never seen anything so beautiful and so strange, she pushes the butcher onto the bed, takes a running leap and lands on top of him.

Pim runs his hands everywhere he can, identifies out loud the shank, the loin chop and the filet mignon—the words make her laugh and then less so when he gets to the thick flank and the haunch. The apprentice's body stiff from days of carving, deboning, and cleaning finally relaxes, softens, his hands decontract, his flesh is pliable, his skin crackles, blood rushes through his veins, he places his fingers on the girl's temples, they're throbbing.

Butchery begins where the animals meet their end, it begins on the outskirts of town, out of sight, far from the butcher shops—it begins at the slaughterhouse.

This year the apprentices have two scheduled visits, blood rituals and baptisms by fire, somewhere between feverish apprehension and impatience. Pim is dreading the ordeal, learning how an animal goes from carcass to edible substance won't be insignificant, witnessing the killing won't be without consequence.

It's time to enter the tragic and secret citadel. It's still dark out when all the students cram into a large van that will take them to the Collinée slaughterhouse, across twenty-four miles of dark road. Pim dozes off, head sliding against the cold window, jacket collar turned up, they're all picturing it, the slaughterhouse, what's behind the scenes, on their way to meet the invisible guardians of meat; they'll need strong stomachs, there'll be cries and the long and dizzying bleeding.

Before the visit, the apprentices gather in the multi-purpose room for a viewing of *Blood of the Beasts*, the Georges

Franju film shot in the slaughterhouses of Pantin in 1949, at the end of the track, where the cattle trains are parked. They watch the former boxing champion of France, all divisions, eviscerate animals, cig in mouth, the heat of spilled blood forming thick steam that the early-morning chill freezes into a toxic fog, they watch a worker cleave his steer with a saw as the clock strikes noon, nuns from the neighboring convent come to collect fats for cooking, cosmetics, and the odd home repair, broad-shouldered men who wield a sledgehammer or an English hammer before expertly inserting a wooden rod into the hole punched through the animals' skulls, rummaging for the spinal cord, and bringing on death. Workers decapitate calves barehanded as they whistle, tossing the heads to a corner of the room where they stack up like a pile of fleshy rubble. The heads have been chopped off, the hooves severed, but the bodies, still twitching, strapped to a workbench, rocked by spasms, bear witness to the final movements of a life now purely vegetative, the last maddened reflexes of the stripped animal, the meat screams and Pim wishes he could rip his ears off.

Some years later, in 1964, a law is passed mandating that animals be completely inert at the time they are bled. Then it is made illegal to suspend an animal before it has been anesthetized. There will be no more blood drinkers, fashionable vampires descending en masse in the wee hours after a night of revelry, come to claim their glass of fresh hemoglobin, the blood of a just-slaughtered animal, gulped down head back to revive their exhausted bodies saturated with alcohol, sex, and dancing, come at dawn all the way to the outskirts of Paris to imbibe a bevy of benefits and iron and leave calmed, energized, senses tingling, skin electrified, minds clear.

Gone are the days when you could bang at the slaughterhouse doors, the sun just barely risen, to claim your dose of blood and vitality. Gone are the days when a dancer from the Opéra de Paris, after twisting her ankle while executing a *saut de chat*, is immediately brought to Pantin to soak her leg in still warm calf viscera. The dancer waits, bored, ankles in the pewter basin, until she feels the swelling go down, the pain diminish, and leaves an hour later light on her feet, her natural cheerfulness, the ritual, and the blood having triumphed over injury.

Pim watched the film in shock, unable to look away, the way you watch a vampire or horror film. Nowadays slaughterhouses are modern, and yet the decapitated bodies still tremble. Nowadays things are different, Pim convinces himself, and yet he'll still have to face the gush of blood, our Pim who thus far has only known firm flesh.

The apprentices report to the slaughterhouse entrance at 5:00 a.m. A vague smell of greasy bacon hovers in the air. The slaughterhouse is in fact a group of metal warehouses spread out across 420 acres of grass. The dumbstruck butchers are standing before one of the largest meat factories in Europe, 2,000 workers alternating day and night.

The first trucks enter the massive parking lot, loaded with pigs. They'll leave with cuts of meat, ready to be delivered to all the Leclerc supermarkets in France.

Every night it's the proletariat of the animal kingdom that is unloaded at the slaughterhouses—plebeian livestock intended to feed the planet, utilitarian and productive animals, unlike the useless poodle, or the hamster that's at best entertaining. Pim feels more affinity with the pig than the dog, more affection for the cow than for the cat, greater respect for the calf than for the parakeet.

The apprentices follow the procession of morning workers who clock in between 5:20 and 5:29 a.m., and who'll clock out at 12:30 p.m. They'll keep the same schedule, make their way up the chain, pass through the refrigeration, stock, and carving rooms, the tripery and the guttery, and the salting station. They'll meet veterinarians and the sanitary inspection staff, the cleaning and maintenance crew, the employees who process and store by-products.

For the time being, the small group advances stiffly, in silence, awed and terrified by the immensity of the site, the alternation of calm and chaos, the smell of smoke, the omnipresent metal. The apprentices stop at the locker room, where they slip on coveralls, blue plastic aprons, chain mail, rubber boots, paper hygiene caps, hard hats, sleeves, and gloves—a surgical ensemble that transforms them into anonymous and technical shapes that disappear beneath layers of sterile rubber. Workers still brittle with sleep remove their everyday clothes (jeans, sweats, leather jackets) and put on fleece sweaters, alpine thermal underwear, and long johns, beneath their white jumpsuits, to protect themselves from the air-conditioning that flows down their spines like ice water and seeps in everywhere as soon as they stop moving. Unhurried pig-keepers and renderers, their expressions mulish and reluctant, who still smell of cigarettes rapidly smoked at the factory entrance, that last asthmatic drag taken before inserting your card into the time clock. Their pockets are filled with chocolate bars, dried apricots, and Nicorette gum.

The decor is stainless steel, fluorescent lighting, and tile flooring; drains, pressure washers, and conveyor belts. In the first room, an overpowering din, hellish in fact—it's not the animals screaming yet but human voices amid the clanging of pneumatic machines, saws, and hooks.

34

The smell is strong and indefinable, a mix of sweat and rancid fat, ammonia and charred pork bristles, bile and rubber. Soon they'll have to enter the killing room, they know it's coming. The sacrificial priest's stage where the animals are hung—a butcher's hook in the tendon—and where the apprentices will watch the blood disappear down the drains, dispersed immediately by a constant hose stream that transforms it into red foam.

The slaughterhouse is a waste factory: liquid effluents redirected to the municipal water treatment plant, solid waste removed daily by leakproof trucks and transported to rendering plants. There is as much cleaning as there is killing in the slaughterhouse, as much waste removal as meat production, as much bleaching as bleeding. The workers obsessively scrub their food-processing boots, repeatedly subjecting the white rubber to a round brush that removes layers of bile and shit as blood and water continue to flow endlessly in an intertwined dribble and at the end there's an ocean that will swallow us all. Pim wonders if all blood has the same smell, animal and human alike. The color varies of course, from scarlet red to a red that's nearly black, but the smell must be universal.

Pim hasn't entered the killing room yet but the blood is already taking over, a massive wave, everything goes red; he's seeing things, a dizzy spell of sorts, some would somatize at less. A thick blanket of swirling garnet envelops him little by little, sinks behind his eyes, penetrates his nostrils and eardrums, drips down his thighs. He doesn't feel good, he'd like a good scrubbing too, a turn under the high-pressure hose so he'll stop hallucinating, he wishes someone would get him out of here.

The instructor's voice tears the apprentice from his apocalyptic visions: *Hygiene conditions here are much more radical than in a butcher shop; for example, wood-handled knives, which can transport germs, are banned, and each blade is cleaned in chlorinated water at 160 degrees.*

The boy regains his sight, the red is gone, Pim pulls himself together, takes a deep breath, and promises himself he won't puke in the first pail of offal that goes by.

Now the apprentices are entering the pork section, this time you can hear the screams echoing across the lairage pens, the animals are agitated, they're angry, their oinking loud and harrowing, the obscene hysteria of 600 hogs slaughtered every hour, 6,000 every day and just as many cows, a frenzy of bellows. It's necessary, beyond necessary, thinks Pim, but how revolting. Rows of hogs pass by, bellies open, suspended from rails, pitiful prey swaying from hooks, shaved from head to tail. The smell of toasted rind mixes with that of the gas leaking from the pigs' gaping stomachs. Pim feels the nausea rising again, it's almost dizzying.

The hogs stream by slowly before the apprentices' frozen gaze, disemboweled clones with pallid hides, then, suddenly, a ghost: Pim thinks he recognizes one of them, he's positive in fact. Pim is hallucinating a pig, an inhabitant of Dubout's Farm, a sprawling hog ranch off the thruway, just outside of Ploufragan. Dubout raises his 1,200 hogs on slatted floors in pens with individual troughs. Pim visited the ranch earlier this year. That morning he had noticed one pig in particular: the animal stood still as he approached, turned its large pink head toward Pim, took a good long look, like it was teasing him, then blinked (English scientists are studying pigs' ability to lie, so why not tease). Its deep-set pupils were round and bright, black pearls, its snout partially covered with a port-wine stain, like a birthmark. Pim had stretched out his hand and scratched the creature's head between the ears, it licked his fingers like an obedient dog then began cackling like a hyena. Not the nasal grunting of a hog but a cascade of strident cries.

Do you have any idea what's in store for you, piggy? Are you playing dumb or plotting a revolution?

This pig was two months old when it encountered Pim. The animal was to be fattened until the 200th day following its birth, at which point it would have attained its maximum weight of 240 pounds. In the subsequent twenty days the pig would be underfed, and on day twenty-one it would fast, the better to arrive in shape, nimbly trotting, plump but not excessively so, fat evenly distributed. Finally, on the 222nd day of its life, it would be brought to the slaughterhouse. This pig is named René. Pim remembers René and today is the 222nd day. We love our animals and we also eat them.

Pim watches the pig hurtle along its unstoppable trajectory, wishes he could shout at the worker to halt the chain, stop the massacre, to save René who has already been slaughtered.

He thought he'd forgotten the pig but his image had buried itself deep in his retinas and now it's reemerging upside down, as cold meat. René is no longer an anonymous pig among the fourteen million piled up across the whole of Brittany, he's no longer one cut out of the seventy-seven pounds of pork consumed annually by every French citizen, he's Pim's pig and how Pim wishes he could have saved him from the industrial breeding complex to give him a better life, basking in the hay, in the warmth of compost rather than on viscous manure. He would have taken the time to fatten him up on a small plot of land even as, at the other end of the world, in Canada, the land of moose, they're manufacturing modern pigs, transgenic pigs, on experimental farms with fluorescent lighting: mice genes are transplanted into pigs and bingo, the large creatures digest better, fatten up more quickly, shit out less phosphorous and pollute less. A mouse crossbred with a pig = better bowel movements. Mice are incredible, they can do everything, but no one in France eats them.

René the pig has now disappeared at the end of the assembly line. Pim raises his hand, part goodbye wave, part apology, but aborts the gesture at the terrifying, inescapable sight of the hogs shaking and trembling, backs quivering, muscles paralyzed, eyes rolling backward, tongues lolling, snouts twitching, heads chopped, guts tumbling, once-living creatures peeled like bananas, a forest of animals hanging from their feet, animals missing their heads but still recognizable, hogs without heads and robbed of the breath of life once exhaled through their nostrils but hogs all the same.

Whereas Pim, without a head, would be unidentifiable. People are heads but animals are bodies, we cut off animals' heads then sometimes we eat them sliced thin and served with vinaigrette. Back in the day, women and men had their heads cut off, too, and the head that rolled off the scaffold was no different than a cow's head or a pig's head, it was a head of flesh and bone that landed in the waiting basket before being grabbed by its hair by the executioner and brandished before the crowd. And then the decapitated body lying to the side was nothing more than a corpse.

Now the pig heads are lined up on a stainless-steel table, the severed feet are over there, arranged in a row, the rumps hang in bunches, the tongues are waiting, suspended as far as the eye can see like a column of soldiers before roll call, the ears are piled in perfect little mounds. Everything is organized and symmetrical, like sausage meat being slowly pushed out of tubes, smooth and consistent. The air is thick and humid. Pim is uncomfortable.

Amid the knackers and the tripists, he's the one with clean hands, he's spared the ingratitude of spilled blood. Amid the countless bodies, he's dizzy again and this time Pim swoons, it's all too much.

First the eyes rotate into their sockets, perform a loop-the-loop and retract, sucked behind the ocular sockets, turning 180 degrees on themselves, your skull is dark, you can't see a thing or else just a tiny point of bright light floating somewhere in your brain, but then you feel yourself leaving, the eyes are white now, rolling back, your eyelids spasm, your head is heavy as an anvil, your feet give way, you're floating in a stifling ocean, dull noises beach like jellyfish in your eardrums, white flashes streak across your retinas, your ears are buzzing, everything is so far, opaque, and here it comes, Pim is slipping away, it's the eyes that slip away first followed by the rest of his body, orbiting the carcasses, he's flying, he's gliding, he's melting, he's gently dissolving, as tender as a Rocky Mountain oyster.

Pim faints, three slaps, a drop of mint liqueur on a sugar

cube and he's up, staggering, *Come on kid, on your feet, this is just the beginning*. It's going to be a long visit.

Pim tells himself he escaped the worst, that clearly it's better to be a butcher, the guy at the end of the chain, the guy who sells the animal minus the parts that make it one, no hide, no head, no feet—just thinking about it makes him feel better. Pim knows everything there is inside an animal, the endless avalanche of innards, but he also knows grassy meadows, the breeder's gentle caress, the veal escalopes to come, and then there's all the people who will eat them, there's the great chain of life, uninterrupted and unavoidable, there's the theory of evolution, the secrets of nature and all of humankind that needs to be fed, there's one world and animals were here before us. Pim thinks about this and a surge of warmth floods his chest, spreads throughout his body, his face reddens, this time it's his emotions getting to him.

Around him workers are hustling and bustling, rhythm accelerating as their muscles warm up, bloodstains on their coveralls, necks drenched in sweat. They shout, run, holler, orders are given and received, an occasional argument, some dirty jokes, some singing, *Am I rough enough? Am I rich enough? I'll never be your beast of burden*, their pace is extraordinary, their movements blindingly fast, they're elbow-deep in viscera, knives slicing and gloved hands digging deep, the vats

41

runneth over. On Christmas Eve, the tradition is to hold a food fight with scraps from the tripery then clink glasses around a buffet where triangles of soft bread covered with slices of sausage the workers have just prepared await.

Among the crew there's Patrick, who takes a few minutes out of his break to talk to the apprentices, Patrick who back in the day always smelled of dead animals, who would delicately separate flesh from meat with a lancet sharper than a razor. He did this to music, had set up a stereo system with a tarp to protect it from spills. He would play a little soft music for the animals he had to kill, the best of Mozart, a compilation of Buddhist mantras or Gregorian chants. Patrick always saw to it that the animals were slaughtered painlessly and to music, one after the next, taking his time, the time needed so that it was done right, so that it was *clean*. Patrick says that way back when, in rural civilizations, whoever slaughtered the animal would first place a coin in its mouth. If they didn't have any coins they would create a totem in the animal's image. The unrelenting pace and constant surveillance prevent Patrick from making similar small effigies but he thinks about it, thinking about it is already something.

Patrick maintains that the problem is not so much killing the animal but knowing how and why we kill it. Not gratuitously, as a distraction or to get rid of its body.

It's a hard and dangerous occupation but it has to be done, because a man's gotta eat and so does everyone else. Feed the progressive and carnivorous human species, a species ever-growing and that needs to be served. Let's thank those who got stuck with the job, the rest of us wouldn't be so brave, we lack the skills and we're staying out of sight.

Beneath his coveralls, at the neckline, there's a visible choker. A necklace of pigs' teeth, caveman-style. Patrick didn't ask permission to keep the teeth but he boldly wears his gems anyway. He's different, his status at the slaughterhouse is special. They say he's been a little off since the accident, that it changed him. Two years ago he was violently kicked in the face by an agitated, untamable cow, a Charolais. Patrick collapsed, unconscious and head bleeding. The EMTs took twenty minutes to show up, the emergency doctor opted for a helicopter evacuation to Saint-Brieuc Hospital, where Patrick underwent three reconstructive surgeries. He became taciturn, hesitant, but didn't want to give up the slaughter-house. So they gave him a new job. He's always dreamed about working with animals, it's a calling. He likes their touch and used to pet the cows in the cattle shed before they were slaughtered, even though it was strongly discouraged—*can't go getting attached to the livestock*. Whenever he stunned a steer, he would whisper, *God is great, God is good, let us thank him for this food*. At the time they offered him a promotion, and even a switch to the office, but Patrick wanted to stay on the livestock side and perfect his art. Today he cleans the carcasses with pressure jets.

A few days after the visit to the slaughterhouse, it's a stormy night, Pim dreams not that a cow kicks him in the face but that a suspended pig falls on his head. In the dream, Pim is a worker at the slaughterhouse, his right arm sore from raising it toward the hanging animals. A doctor approaches, his silhouette is hazy at first then it comes into focus: a white coat, a physician's bag, and wire-rimmed glasses. Pim extends his hand in greeting but the pig lurching overhead suddenly slips off its hook and drops, smashing into the apprentice butcher before he can shake the doctor's hand. The pig bounces like a ball, continues its trajectory through the factory, then rolls into the poultry shed, out of view.

There was an earlier incident of a pig slipping off its hook and landing on a slaughterer, crashing onto the worker's shoulders with the full force of its weight. Because of a hook poorly inserted into the animal's hoof, an overly wide gap between the knee and thigh tendons, because of ripped flesh and the lack of a safety protocol.

In the sanitation area, his dysfunctional tear ducts act up again, Pim's eyes brim over with tears impossible to hold back as the instructor explains how to remove marrow. *Watch closely: you grab the marrow with the tip of your knife, press the blade against the spinal column that has been sawn in half, then you cut all the fibers that are holding it. Next, toss the marrow in a separate vat, it's SRM, Specified Risk Material, there's all kinds of crap that could be hiding in there. And ever since mad cow disease we incinerate everything, bone marrow, tonsils, spleen, even the intestines. Soon we'll be equipped with a semiautomated machine for the de-marrowing, there'll be a mechanism to suck out the spinal cord, it'll go a lot faster. Hey no need to cry, kid, don't you feel all right? You'll never become a butcher if you can't handle this stuff.*

It's nothing, sir, I'm fine, it's a disease actually, nothing I can do about it, the crying starts on its own.

Nobody believes in this disease, since the beginning, nobody's believed it.

HISTORY OF THE INDUSTRIALIZED SLAUGHTERHOUSE

At first slaughterhouses were public, then they went private: butchery was industrialized, the decision made to kill by assembly line, to regulate how animals died, to safeguard this ancestral rite against individual whim and improvisation.

When history began, the history of carnivorous humanity, man killed the animal he ate, man was a hunter; we, man and beast, were intimately acquainted. I'd spot the creature in the wild, then track, slaughter, butcher, and swallow it. Come winter I'd throw its hide over my naked, vulnerable body. An offering from it to me, a private affair of sorts, just between us. I no longer eat animals I've killed myself, someone or something else does it for me, the intermediaries ever multiplying. In truth nobody really kills animals anymore, not since the invention of assembly-line slaughter: this mechanized labor is inattentive, it's irresponsible, and death is divided up.

———

Detroit, Autumn 1913: Ford introduces the first assembly line to manufacture the Model T. But assembly-line work wasn't created to assemble cars, it was invented to take apart animals. In the mid-nineteenth century, the slaughterhouse of the city of Chicago introduces its first cutting and packing assembly line, testing the first technical solution to the challenge of mass production.

In Chicago, aka Porkopolis, large factories sprout up and process thirteen million animals a year. Hogs file past on conveyor belts—this worker cleans the ears, that one removes the bristles—and the carcasses are hung from an overhead crane, gently sloping rails leading from one station to the next, the worker grabs an animal, brings down the bacon. A brilliant idea: transport animal-objects by suspending them in the air.

The workers often have their own bright ideas, to make the job easier, to improve conditions, to ease and optimize their labor. They invent machines, the assembly line, but also, for example, a machine to extract pig fat to make margarine. The workers of Chicago's slaughterhouses are ingenious, soon they'll even unionize.

President Hoover promises his fellow citizens a chicken in every pot, they'll need to pick up the pace if he's going to keep his word. The hogs that entered the packinghouse a few hours earlier emerge as hams, sausages, lard lotion, and Bible covers. The bits and pieces leave via a tiny railway that winds through the factory and leads to freight cars chilled by huge blocks of ice, then it's the conquest of the West, trains of meat crossing America, soon they'll cross the ocean and after World War II, American farmers will feed the whole world.

Pim and the apprentices have reached the cattle section, the elite, the cream of the crop—that's just how it is, the cow will always be the noble, sacred animal, the hog will always be the pleb, the shit-stirrer that wakes up the whole neighborhood, screaming and squealing like a stuck pig.

The bovines are ceremoniously escorted off the truck then gathered in the cattle shed. The animals are gently but firmly pushed along by their haunches, *Let's go ladies need to make room for everyone*. The cowherds take care with their charges, calm their bellowing with big friendly pats on the neck, give them water to calm their anxiety (or more likely to ensure their meat is light and appetizing). The delivery is monitored, the accompanying paperwork and ear tags verified, then the animals are placed in lairage until the following information has been recorded: certification label, place of birth, place of fattening. Every one of France's 100 million bovines. *Where do you come from, sweetheart? What did you graze on? Which lush pastures have you been trampling all these years? What kind of field did you tear up with your nervous, impatient hooves? And what type of breeder did you have? The I-know-the-name-of-every-one-of-my-cows type or the feedlot-steaks-on-legs type? I get the feeling you were well-loved, my little Holstein.*

This is where our paths part, you know, the staff and the animals never take the same hallway, can't be consorting with the commoners—kidding! C'mon don't pout, you're too sensitive, it's for safety is all. I go this way, and you, you go that way, toward the scald, you'll see that it's a little snug, though, actually, it's a trap.

The cow is in the trap but things don't always go as planned and without warning she licks the killer's face, she's the one giving the kiss of death, she licks his neck, forehead, cheeks, but she's not done yet, this is tenderness, this is love, the animal's massive raspy and muscular tongue pushes the man against a wall, corners him, a cow violating a slaughterer, she's still licking, her head is now pressed against the worker's chest, she rubs and keeps rubbing, the man is distraught, stroking an animal on the head is all it takes—you can no longer kill it.

Pim flinches when he hears the bang: the animal is stunned by a shot from a captive bolt pistol at its forehead, the most pliable part of the skull, at the intersection of two lines the slaughterer mentally draws on the animal's head. To ensure that the cow falls correctly, he guides her to put her weight on the correct hoof, the creature's neck twists backward, she falls on her horns then chest and finally the right flank. The slaughterer places one finger on the cow's eye to make sure the eyelid doesn't move, proof she's been knocked out. Then the stunned animal is suspended, the carcass begins its circuit; Pim can smell it, a smell of barns, milk, and straw. The worker approaches, face devoid of expression apart from the weariness of the assembly line, a sticking knife worn at his waist like a medieval sword, a knife that he spent a long time whetting before proceeding (to buy some time and breathe a little, since you're allowed to take a break to sharpen your blades), chest forward, legs bowed, he inserts the knife into a fold of flesh on the chest, goes through hair, muscle, and nerves, cuts the carotid arteries, that's where the thick gleaming blood will spurt out the fastest, the strongest, and yes, it erupts in big, loud spurts, in a gush. The cartilaginous white of the trachea is visible now, the skin is nothing, a fragile screen, a frail and alterable shield behind which there's a hell of a mess, a nameless chaos of flesh and viscera. The worker's motions are so steady they won't need to be repeated. He's careful not to plant the blade too deep, to prevent blood from flowing into the stomach. The slaughterer moves the cow's hoof back and forth to facilitate the effusion of blood, it needs to be pumped then collected, then mixed with an anticoagulant.

51

The apprentices are stunned, jaws rigid, green around the gills boys. It's not the sight of blood, more the violence with which it escapes the wound, it's the intensity of the blood, its impatience. It's life breaking free, right in your face, splattering everywhere.

Does the slaughterer truly kill animals without anger and without hate? The apprentices are taught that it's the law of nature. If we breed animals but don't kill them there'll be too many of them and then what would happen? A revolution? An animal uprising? If we didn't kill a billion chickens and forty million rabbits every year, would they join forces to have our hides?

If we don't kill the animals we breed for food, other more ferocious and barbaric creatures will do it in our stead: hyenas, wolves, and bears. Animals are meant to be eaten and we eat them the best way we can. Get that into your head, Pim. But Pim doesn't need convincing, he firmly believes that a sheep is destined to work alongside the shepherd, then it's the slaughterhouse with the slaughterer, otherwise it's the wolf. Maybe if we didn't eat our livestock they would starve to death, simply enough, and Pim isn't unfeeling when it comes to animals.

A few days later the girl from the bench called him. She'd had fun the other night. So they saw each other again, had sex again. Without bothering to chat beforehand, grab a drink in town, or catch a movie. They agreed to meet outside Pim's building, kissed in front of the big double door, he wanted to go upstairs right away, and this time the girl found the experience somewhat mechanical. Gentle, yes, but mechanical. A weird combination, a weird feeling, and the feeling was of kindhearted absence. Once again Pim carved the girl into an anatomical chart as he stroked her body but this time it wasn't quite so funny. She said he was using her, he didn't respond, didn't protest or agree, his hands still delicately kneading her flesh, taking his time, like a presurgical evaluation—Pim was focused, tender, and distant. The girl was enamored and annoyed, angry but not sure why, there wasn't really much to reproach him for. After the sex he suggested a beer but the girl who felt like crying left in silence.

The hardest part's done, the bleeding's over, the animal's gone, vanished, soon there'll be meat, the bleeding's over, we're on the other side now, soon the butcher will enter the scene, let's give him a round of applause, soon it'll be your turn Pim, your spot in the never-ending, all-consuming, self-sustaining slog, filet mignon in the window and pot-au-feu on Sundays.

A few minutes ago it had been right there, an animal tagged with a number; it had been warm and now, if he wanted, Pim could plunge his hand inside the cold meat. The transformation into a carcass happened right before his eyes, he's preparing to watch the animal be eviscerated, carved, and dismembered, he's trembling with anticipation, body electrified. Soon it will be in his hands, an indistinct form ready to be modified anew, it will be transformed into a beef roast, then cooked in its juice and metabolized by a human organism who will digest it more or less quickly, more or less easily, with or without fries.

A few more nervous twitches before the animal stills, another worker cuts off its front hooves, then the gutter extracts the heart, liver, lungs, and bladder. Inertia takes over. A technician applies high-voltage stimulation to the carcass to tetanize the muscles and more easily remove the skin, exercising delicacy and dexterity to keep the former from touching the latter. The detached skin hangs like an apron or a dress flowing at the animal's feet. The worker ties off the rectum so that the contents of the digestive system don't escape, at least not by that channel. A second technician, facing the first one, removes the udders. They look like twins symmetrically working the carcass, you take the front right hoof, I'll take the front left hoof, together they hang the carcass by the ankles, guide the cow into a brisk, faultless choreographed number (poultry are hung by their feet too. Because they get stressed, they're taken at night, the breeders are woken at an ungodly hour, and the chickens are abducted under cloak of darkness, they're placed in crates, the sun has yet to rise, and the workers handle them in the dark beneath an ultraviolet light).

Now the skinned animal is blanketed in greasy foam; a man steps forward and delicately wipes it away with a blade. When no one is looking, Pim runs his finger over the carcass and tastes the sleek flesh. It's acrid and pungent, a violent flavor that seeps into his mouth like a poison, *fuck that's nasty*. He spits into his hands to get rid of the taste, then wipes them on the tails of his coat, he'd been hoping for something similar to freshly ground steak tartare, he's worried about this meat that seems to have already spoiled. At the end of the line, an agent from the regional office of veterinary services inspects the carcass. Under his white coat, the thick knot of his tie signals that he's not a member of the working class. He collects the obex, the tiny V-shaped piece of the brain stem where mad cow disease can be detected. The sample is sent to the lab for analysis, a sanitary procedure required since the outbreak.

The outbreak that won't be forgotten anytime soon. Those first televised images of funeral pyres, England assembling its cattle by the thousands and burning them, then the European Community and its embargo on British meat, France demanding declarations of any cases of bovine spongiform encephalopathy. This time mankind went too far, we gave animal-based flours to herbivores, made animal feed out of animal powder, we invented a new kind of cannibalism and then: fear mounting and death lurking, animals fall then men, meat consumption crashes, nobody dares take a bite of our animal brethren, henceforth tracked and identified, their origins posted in butcher shops and restaurants—a public health tool and precautionary measure, now man and cow look at each other with fear in their eyes, everyone is under suspicion, the mood is grim.

Pim and the others follow the line and the workers' dance transformation by transformation. Dressed in the same protective gear, they can be distinguished from the employees by their hunched shoulders and dangling arms, their sluggishness, the way they follow the instructor from station to station, sleepwalking almost, dragging their sneaker-clad feet, looking lost: *Note that evisceration must begin at the latest forty-five minutes after the slaughter. Any longer and the intestines become porous and the enzymes and microorganisms they contain can leak out, reach the muscles, and contaminate the carcass. You need to be especially vigilant at this stage. Everyone got that?* They nod yes, listless and resigned.

Several feet away, the offal is removed. Pim wonders if there are ever any surprises when you open up a cow. One might imagine something never-before seen, something unexpected, spurting from the entrails, a random object or a ray of light, an odd item the cow might have eaten, a piece of a fruit tree, a clock, a beguiling perfume, an old book with riddles to solve, a photo of its mother, an accidentally swallowed chicken feather—because a feather can kill a cow, which is why, on farms, poultry are kept separate from cattle. But no, it's always the same green, mushy innards, no revelation, no hidden treasure, always the same old sticky mess inside the animal, no portentous sign, no sack of gold in lieu of the stomach and congratulations you've won yourself a tropical vacation. Just a knotwork of intestines and pipes, disappointing really.

And yet that would have compensated for the arduousness of the job: waking up at 4:45 a.m. to sort the offal and run it through the vacuum packer. The pieces pass by on a conveyor belt, white offal on one side—head, feet, stomach; red offal on the other—heart, liver, tongue, brain, spleen, lungs, thymus. The worker's wearing huge blue plastic gloves that go up to her elbows and protect her forearms from getting soiled. She started on the assembly line at nineteen, now she's twenty-eight and has already had two operations for carpal tunnel.

For the first time, Pim sees himself at the top of the social ladder, a baron among the commoners. He might have thought: the workers and I are on the same side, both down-and-out, both elbow-deep in the same meat, in the same shit. But instead he thinks: I'm special, I'm on the right side, of meat and of fate. He doesn't feel solidarity. Sympathy, yes, empathy even, but not solidarity. He understands the link, he's grateful, but all of it feels very distant, the strident noise of the band saw cutting the carcass in half feels distant. And yet, at the end of the line, where the halving occurs, the final step in the chain, Pim is now looking at two pieces that closely resemble the half- or quarter-carcasses delivered every week to Morel's butchery. In his head and very quickly he goes through all the steps, starting from when the animals reach the slaughterhouse, that led to this moment when he finally recognizes the meat. A collection of actions that made an extraordinary metamorphosis possible—a cow becomes a steak, you won't believe your eyes. On the Renault assembly line they make cars out of scraps of metal. Here it's the opposite, they produce scraps of meat from breathing machines. They chop and grind, they don't put together they take apart, they don't assemble they dismantle. The workers have taken a vow of poverty, pallid and bloodstained beneath the industrial lighting, they're feeding the whole of France—*and you're not gonna fill all those bellies with three sows per breeder and no factories.*

At the slaughterhouse everything comes to a halt—time, life, animals. Pim watches the carcasses move past, bisected animals hung ass to ass by the hundreds, weighed, labeled, washed, and there's a twinge in his heart not unlike the brutal effect of a cooling agent, a shot of emotion and adrenaline; the carcasses are making their way to chilling rooms where they will be drained of their moisture, their temperatures will progressively decrease, their muscles will slacken upon contact with oxygen. Soon their tender fibers will be crushed by expert fingers, the fingers of Pim the butcher.

The visit is over, the apprentices' stomachs are rumbling, their eyes red with fatigue and from what they've seen, their bodies worn out, haunted looks on their faces. Leaving the factory, the noise, the cold, the fluorescent lights and the smells, returning to the clear vast sky, the greenery, is a shock, sudden hyperventilation, blindness, the painful beauty of nature rediscovered, out in the open. As though they'd been living for days on end inside a screeching, clammy box, roiling and rolling under the influence of violent psychotropics. The apprentices scatter across the lawn that surrounds the factory, pull their lunches out of their backpacks, cast a wary eye at their ham sandwiches, discreetly peeking between the pieces of bread to get a good look at the pig now in slices, then take a big bite, they're starving, gazes lost in the distance.

Pim sits apart from the others. He wants to go back, he's plotting a nocturnal break-in, an illicit visit, not to discover the rooms shielded from view, all the nasty things, the countless secrets, that might be hidden inside, but to go down the line again, start over alongside the animals, take the same corridors, follow them closely, on his knees, head down, bare feet in the blood, to see what it's like to be a beast of burden.

Pim creeps through the grass, his long shadow like a snake on the ground, he reaches the swine building, in this moment feeling more solidarity with the pigs than with the workers, closer to these unloved hogs that stink, screech, and all look alike, these unruly, stubborn creatures cursed with weak hearts. Pim is focused on the hogs. He's hoping he'll blend in all the easier since pigs have a biological and anatomical makeup very similar to that of humans; they can even get sunburned, ever since they lost their boar bristles. Pim inches into a passel (the pigs arrive at the slaughterhouse in breeding groups, which are never mixed; each farm group hates the others and can become violent), a group of fifty-some animals squealing as they are unloaded from the truck. Still crouching and anonymous amid these frightened creatures paying him no mind, far too busy wondering how to save their skins, he enters the enclosure where they will be spray-washed and fed. Their hides are as pink as an ass in springtime, maybe Pim should get naked to better blend into the pink, to avoid getting spotted, namely by the pigs, who are terrified of strangers. Strangers are stressful and these creatures are very sensitive to stress, they worry over nothing; even the fattest hog in the world, a one-ton Chinese specimen, is as skittish as a baby seal. Though how can we measure the exact degree of their stress, or evaluate their pain? Pigs cry but how can we know if it's terror, because they don't recognize their surroundings, because they've been moved? Are they sweating? Trembling? Are their heart rates accelerating? Pim presses his ear against the snout of the first pig that passes in the hope of measuring its respiratory rate, he presses his fingers to the base of its neck to check its blood pressure. A blood test would be helpful too, to know its adrenaline levels, and so would shining a light in its eyes. But the pig being examined violently pulls away and sends Pim flying into a barrier. Despite the noise the apprentice still hasn't been discovered, it's a miracle, or else nobody wants to see it, a tall young man in the middle of the pigpen no thank you.

Now Pim and his companions are sliding onto conveyor belts that carry them to the restraint boxes. They're misted with water to calm their nerves, a little cool refreshment before anesthesia by electronarcosis. Fear affects the quality and taste of the meat, the distressed pig produces an acid that decomposes muscle, its acid-permeated flesh turns white and pasty, and there's no reason to add to the anxiety of a pig that hasn't hurt anyone, or to inflict mediocre food on the consumer. The first candidate hurtles onto a rubber mat and concludes its journey in the killing zone. The hatch door is locked behind the pig to protect its brethren, so as not to perturb them unnecessarily. Pim presses one eye against the perforated metal barrier and can make out the hands of a worker placing electrified pincers on each side of the animal's head. It falls, struck dumb. Back in the day, pigs were knocked out with a mallet to the forehead, back in the day, *boudins* were made in the farmyard: four liters of blood per bled animal. The cut couldn't be too narrow, which would require a second stab, or too wide, which would make the blood spurt out everywhere with a great deal going to waste. The blood was gathered in a bucket and beaten by hand so it didn't curdle, then it was chilled, that was the tradition. If Pim was a pig, that wouldn't be his choice. Better to go with an industrial, hygienic, and collective slaughter than a clumsy and clandestine killing in an unsanitary farmyard.

Pim manages to slide off the conveyor belt that leads to the slaughter. Still invisible, quick as an eel, he creeps inside the dehairing room. The pigs are hung by their hindquarters, hams in the air, then scratched and scalded with hot water. With a whistle the knacker gives the command for the rotary machines and there go the scrapers, beating, rubbing, and burning off the remaining bristles. Soon the pigs will be hairless. Pim, who's now also naked, takes a running start, grabs the first hook that goes by, joins the carousel and gets his back scratched, washed, and scrubbed by impassive workers who, after seeing the same pink shapes streaming past all day long, can no longer tell a nose from a snout, a pig from a man in briefs when the man's hanging from his toes, who simply think, when Pim goes by, this one's a bit thin isn't it, not good for much except Hot Pockets filling. But it's high time that Pim, terrified, let go and drop to the ground: the pig suspended in front of him has been cleaved into a massive buttonhole, from groin to neck, split in two against the clamor of an electric saw.

Pim rolls along the floor, avoiding the viscera hurtling down like bombs dropping from the sky. And there's plenty of those guts spurting out, because everything is good in the pig, everything is good in the pig except its squeal, everything is good though the pig is good for nothing apart from being eaten—at least sheep can offer their wool and chickens their feathers. Then come, in succession, the hoof removers, the ham hock cleavers, and the tail cutters.

The worst avoided, Pim curls up in a ball in a corner, body covered with meat shrapnel, he's trembling, still invisible to the world, of animal and man alike, he looks around for the clothes he left at the entrance, wants to get dressed without being seen. He's already regretting the insanity of his plan, would rather forget about it now, avoid the fatal moment—the killing. Pim is afraid of blood when it's warm and moving. He spares a thought to the animals, who are perhaps no longer animals, transformed by man through the millennia, selected, manipulated, crossbred, less living things than metabolic factories, edible laboratories, organic inventions used to feed the human species. Pim feels tears rising and these ones are tears of confusion. It's time to get out of this mess, get dressed and fast, and leave the factory a second time without being spotted. He continues crawling until he reaches his clothes, pulls on his jeans with his back glued to the floor, then his sweater, his sneakers, springs up and runs like mad toward the exit. *You there!* He speeds up, a man in a white coat on his heels, *Stop or I'll call the police!* his long legs carry him far, he disappears through an emergency exit, leaves the factory behind him and races ahead through the fields.

Pim is the second living creature to escape the Collinée slaughterhouse. The first was, in fact, a pig. The hog house getaway, a famous story shared at every town celebration and family gathering, an anecdote told to the newbies, a legendary incident rehashed going on ten years. The pig made a run for it. Because pigs, after being manipulated for so long, have become cunning as foxes. This one took off when the livestock truck was being unloaded. The hog bolts, swift as a hare, knocking over everything in its path, a hare but also a bull, a buffalo willing to destroy everything and who squeezes through a swinging door, belly to the ground, straight ahead direction freedom with no hesitation despite the labyrinthine configuration of the factory. The fresh air filtering into the slaughterhouse corridors guides the pig to the exit, the workers try to catch him midflight but he slips through their fingers, someone leaps onto the hog with arms spread wide only to tumble off, another grabs his tail, he's dragged several feet, the worker lets go, nobody dares plant a knife in the animal's back to slow him down, nothing can stop him, it's the great escape, and finally the pig's outside, he cuts across the parking lot, past the metal gates, and now it's the regional highway stretching into infinity, cars zigzagging to avoid him, a scooter swerves abruptly and ends up in a ditch, the pig gallops toward town temples pounding, keeps up the pace, how is it possible for a pig to run as fast as a greyhound? Saliva foams in the corner of his mouth, his tongue is flapping like a flag against jowls drawn back by sheer velocity, his ears are flattened, his snout wet and red from exertion, then the runaway cuts through some fields, reaches the town limits, passes the first traffic signs, the roundabout, charges anyone who tries to get in his way, aims for an opening in the roadway, a black chasm that sucks him in, home free at last, the pig jumps eyes closed ass over hooves, Alice tumbling down her hole, bounces, slips, continues his mad dash, and takes refuge in a sewer canal: the pig is hidden. Except now the pig is trapped at a bottleneck after clumsily running nearly a third of a mile through the reeking, viscous underground darkness. Fat pig stuck in a pipe and can't take another step.

The jailbreak is reported, witnesses saw the animal crossing at the red light, a young woman swears the road swallowed him up, *the street opened and hand to God the pig fell in the hole*. The municipal maintenance services, with backup from the regional public works department, think they can free the animal by forcing him to go backward. The rescue operation commences. They pump high-pressure water through the entire network first, then drop the flares. *What about the dogs? You didn't send in the dogs?* Impossible to liberate the animal. The fire department is called but they don't have any better luck. A fireman attempts to squeeze through the canal but the tunnel becomes dangerously narrow. The firefighters decide on a different approach: they'll talk to the pig, they'll negotiate, why not bring in an animal psychologist, but in the end, exasperated, they start yelling anything and everything at the creature, futilely ordering him to come out. They try to lure him with apple peels but nothing doing, the pig merely grunts and its strident squealing amplified by the echo of the subterranean cavities reaches the town surface in deafening geysers, children wake up and cry out in fear in the middle of the night, squeezing their mother's hand tightly, there's a monster under the cement and it's here to take revenge. After one night of unsuccessful attempts, as the pig grows weaker and weaker, as his scream of terror turns into a hoarse, intermittent wheeze, the deputy director of the environment office decides to rip open the road itself in order to free the animal that will otherwise rot there: very early in the morning, an accredited public works company drills into the asphalt, the pig is located and brought to the surface, at the end of his rope, by way of a crane. The large strapped-in creature hangs in the air, apathetic and filthy, the onlookers who have been shuffling around for hours give a fervent round of applause, whistle, shout, everyone wants to touch and hug the miraculous pig survivor, arms stretch past the security rope, police officers raise their voices to keep the crowd back, blinding camera flashes, someone wants a photo of the animal with the new baby, a veterinarian rushes over, pushes back the troop of clustering gawkers with his blue latexed hands; a referendum is improvised: should the pig be saved or sent back to the slaughterhouse? The creature is saved with 88% of the votes, a triumph. He's designated the official mascot, gets a full page in the local paper and a pen for life in the town hall courtyard with a cockade around his neck. Named Steve McQueen, hero of *The Great Escape*. Steve the Pig McQueen.

In any case Steve had become inedible, the traumatic incident had permanently altered the quality of his flesh, rendering it too acidic and unfit for consumption, or perhaps only as thickly breaded and heavily seasoned nuggets.

The year comes to a close and Pim is summoned to the first exam required for his butchery certification: product transformation. This exam evaluates the candidate's aptitude for the preparation of meat, poultry, and tripe products intended for sale.

You will be graded on your ability to organize your work and your mastery of fundamental techniques: meat separation, boning, trimming, nerve removal, barding, tying, and dressing. And on whether you respect rules of hygiene and safety. Please note that the state of your work stations, tools, and materials after each stage will also be evaluated during this exam. Gentlemen, young lady, you have four and a half hours.

Cuts are lined up on Pim's workstation: a pair of flank steaks, a veal shoulder, a lamb fillet, and a barded round beef. Pim has at his disposal a whetstone, a cleaver, and a dozen knives—for cutting, filleting, and nerve removal. He's wearing a coat of mail over a large white cotton apron. His right hand is protected by the same metallic netting. This shining knight cuts a fine figure, he's ready for combat, the grand T-bone tournament, the veal will be easy to bone, its meat as young and tender as the heart of a princess. He grabs the shoulder, cuts off the largest end of the bone then rinses it.

The apprentice is drowning in his houndstooth butcher pants, small beads of sweat forming beneath a white cap. He's wearing a red silk tie, knotted high and tight over a button-down with thin blue stripes, hidden by a canvas worker jacket. The tie squeezes the larynx and hinders concentration, but it's obligatory. A vestimentary tradition, a boastful vanity that's here to stay, the regulation tie signaling a job well done, pride, courtesy, and hygiene (chest hair hidden from view?). Preferably red to hide any eventual stains. The butcher also pushes up his sleeves—make an impression and make it good—arms bared in the cold, a silk knot in a world of blood, virility both barbaric and elegant. The butcher isn't the hea-then who slaughters and dismembers the animal; his work consists of a long succession of operations to deconstruct and reconstruct the carcass, the methodical manipulation of the cadaver, which will be chopped, camouflaged, assembled, and sculpted. The butcher transforms the skinned animal into perfect well-balanced cuts—barded roast, parsley flower, impeccable binding, slipknot, hats off to the artist.

Pim plunges into the meat, singularly focused on his neat, economical movements. He separates the flank steaks, shaves off the remaining hairs, makes sure that not a single piece of flesh is still sticking to the bone, that he doesn't cut into muscle, that he respects the anatomical divisions. The examiner moves quietly through the exam room, briefly leans over Pim's bustling hands, but the young butcher doesn't get distracted.

Pim fully respected the cleaning and disinfection protocol and organized his workspace properly. He scraped and rubbed down his chopping block, eliminated the slightest waste, the most minuscule stain. The workstation is good as new, virginal in fact: not a drop of blood, nothing happened here, no sign of sacrifice, no proof either.

At the end of the four-and-a-half-hour evaluation, Pim stands at attention in front of his immaculate workbench. Smock wrinkled and stained with black blood, oily death stains, faint splatters of scarlet dew, the traces of hands wiped clean, myoglobin-encrusted fingerprints, a trickle of jus winding its way through the folds of cloth, cap pushed back, a pungent, gamy smell of sweat, palms red with blood and effort, swollen fingers: the boy is a butcher.

To obtain his certification, Pim will need to correctly pack and weigh his products, label his products in a logical and visible manner, and pass the final test (supply, organization, and work environment) by answering the following questions:

71

1. *A wholesaler delivers an adult beef half-carcass. You are responsible for accepting the product and stocking it in the cold room. The delivery person hands you some documents. What are they?*
     - *Vehicular hygiene certificate?*
     - *Dated delivery slip?*
     - *Bill for the previous delivery?*
     - *Identification card?*

2. *According to the identification card below, was this Charolais specimen bred in its place of birth? Explain your answer.*

3. *What is the maximum permissible core temperature of the half-carcass upon receipt?*

At the end of the first year of the program, the most deserving students—arbitrarily chosen by the director on the basis of undefined criteria—are offered a one-month internship with an animal breeder. A reward of sorts: the opportunity to improve their understanding of livestock and get some fresh air far from the fridges and white tiling.

Pim is glad to participate because a butcher without a cow is quite the abstraction.

Pim admires those butchers who visit their meat on hooves, who want to stroke its neck, assess the animal as it grazes, judge for themselves, look it in the eye. They drive all the way to the farms to meet their future steaks, they consider it part of the job, know what you're selling, who you're selling. They can tell, just by looking at the beast, as a whole, what it'll be worth stripped down, it's a sixth sense, the butcher who sees through ginger coats and behind snouts.

Pim wouldn't mind getting back to nature, leading the steers to the trough, wielding the pitchfork, turning up earth trampled by the cows, telling them thank you, telling them hello girls, so it was you hanging upside down in the cold room, taking the time to look at them straight on, these animals that toil at our sides to produce milk, eggs, and blood, their collective comestible handiwork, the farm wasn't built in a day though now everything goes faster and faster.

Pim will be hosted by a cattle breeder in Pays de Caux who runs a small farm near Écrainville with approximately one hundred Norman cows. The apprentice butcher will serve as cowherd for a month. He'll be responsible for the day-to-day of the herd: milking, medical care, feed. He'll need to monitor the animals' good behavior and good health: Are they eating well? Which one is ready to calve? Is the herd getting along or not? He'll have to get to know every cow and clean the crud off every ass. First milking of the day between 6:00 and 7:00 a.m., unpredictable night hours (you never know when a cow will give birth), and accommodation provided in the form of a massive 100-square-foot loft that's completely renovated and equipped with a sink.

Pim arrives at the Bréauté-Beuzeville train station with two suitcases and covers the remaining four miles by taxi.

The car enters the muddy path leading to the courtyard of the farm, a nineteenth-century building constructed at a right angle and surrounded by fields pitted by stamping cows, an open grove planted with apple trees, a haystack protected by tarps held down by tractor tires, and, in the background, a long, low stable made of red brick and flint, covered by a zinc roof. Tonight, the animals are being kept inside, dry. It's drizzling, the place looks abandoned, it's milking time, and in the distance you can hear the deep, low notes of mooing.

Pim is venturing into the farmyard in his brand-new green boots when something pops out of the open-air hen house with an earsplitting gobble—a turkey in splashy plumage. Its screech startles Pim, who admires its majestic movements, the over-the-top arrogance of what remains a farm bird, its coloring, the deep black and green of its feathers, the scarlet red of its eruptive, leathery neck. The creature comes closer, curious and friendly, making sounds that Pim doesn't know how to interpret, a call of excitement, the call of a joyful turkey gobble gobble.

Pim is welcomed by the affable turkey first then, a few minutes later, by the unmarried breeder in overalls who sets him down a drink on the wax tablecloth in the large family room. Hard cider and a few slices of supermarket dried sausage reluctantly chewed by Pim. The setup is rudimentary; the only decorative element, a framed photo of a heifer that won the general livestock competition, cattle division, presiding from the china cabinet. The breeder is posing beside his cow and the conversation turns to this prizewinning beast proudly lifting her massive head before the camera: *An excellent contender, 1,500 pounds, her milk production record was 7,275 pounds in 100 days. Not only is she a great dairy cow but she has lots of beef potential. Plus a good pelvis, which means calving should be easy, and a nice topline, perfectly balanced, a clean neck, no really, she has a lot going for her.* Which is why she was awarded a medal, an enamel plaque nailed above the gas stove.

The breeder knows his ninety-some cows by name and tonight lists them one by one to Pim, who takes notes. Minnie, the enterprising runt of the litter who sticks to herself; Valerie, the snobby loudmouth forever slapping the others with her tail; Blue Moo, the A+ student, a bit of a suck-up, always the first to go back into the barn; Pearl, the veteran who knows the routine, blasé even before she's prime for butchering; Brunette, who's mildly compulsive: whenever you change her straw, she systematically follows behind, redoes her little nest, organizes the hay just how she likes it with the tip of her muzzle.

Pim had learned that Normans are the top milk-producing breed in France, number one in protein levels, that they're known for their fertility, longevity, hardiness, and gentle temperament. He already knows that Normans are a dual-purpose breed—they produce milk then, come retirement, meat. The breeder completes Pim's education: a three-month fattening-up period before the slaughterhouse; a diet of fodder, soybean meal, and beet pulp; the cattle are kept in the barn from November to April, the rest of the year in the fields, where they graze eight hours a day and ruminate for ten, which translates to some 100 pounds of grass to digest on the most plentiful days.

The breeder has some of his animals slaughtered at home, his favorites, the ones he doesn't want to part with. He has them killed in the courtyard or in the barn, old-school and by the book, by an itinerant slaughterer. The kind with a knife at his waist, whistling behind the wheel of his utility vehicle, starched apron folded on the rear deck and metallic gloves in their case. He announces his arrival with a honk as he goes through the gate and up the dirt path that leads to the imposing structure. This professional killer makes the rounds of the farms in Normandy, slaughters animals exclusively on-site, at the request of customers who engage his services via text message: *u free 4 pig slaughter?* :) It's more humane at the farm. The animals are less stressed and it's always better to die at home, in your bed or on your straw. The slaughterer gets out of his car slowly, the sky is orange and streaked with thin clouds: jeans, oiled leather boots, and a thick canvas shirt that will soon disappear beneath a sterile jumpsuit.

He's brought before the animal waiting docilely in the farm courtyard, who's then led easily into the barn, the trust all-encompassing. He draws his captive bolt pistol, the breeder looks away, the killer stuns the animal, the animal collapses, the breeder looks back at his cow, then solemnly hands the slaughterer the tractor key: the creature now has to be lifted by the machine so it can be bled at the correct height. Knife drawn emphatically, a single lateral arm movement and it's over. The fatty blood drips onto straw instead of factory cement, absorbed quickly by yellow earth that the breeder turns vigorously with his pitchfork.

Before his first night on the farm, Pim is guided to the stabling area. The building is immense, well-ventilated and clean, lit by a glacial moon that peeks through high-placed windows. The cows are divided along both sides of a large central corridor. The breeder points to the doyenne of the herd: Red Pied, eight years old. *This morning she produced 46 liters.* Her udders, horribly swollen, quiver at the slightest movement, gourds full of milk. Pim wonders if all that weight is painful, all that tension in the lower belly. *Don't start projecting. Don't start thinking they're like us.*

Red Pied lifts her tail and defecates. *Now that's a sign of stress, it's cause she doesn't know you yet. Go on, give her a little scratch, this one loves to be scratched. Take it slow, you can't rush her is all, you gotta be decent with animals, they're living creatures too you know. Just be gentle is all. If the breeder's gentle, the animals are calm, everything is calm. And they won't bother you. You have to understand how animals function and I'm not just talking about their digestive systems. Once you get it, the rest is teamwork.*

Because cows are workers, they build a career alongside the breeder and under his direction. Dogs and tigers don't work, but cows? Cows grind and produce. They are tiny breathing factories, four-legged milk/meat mills that never clock out.

Dogs provide company, tigers are beautiful, swift, and cruel, cows aren't always graceful in their movements but they are profitable, raised to be fattened and slaughtered (and that's time spent together), raised to be eaten but not just, and when I eat you little cow, when I devour you at the end of the story, it won't take away any of the beauty or joy or connection. Little cow, I will love you as long as I eat you.

Pim goes up to his loft room, opens the window, and sticks out his head: the darkness is star-speckled and deep, the air invigorating and fragrant, a smell of slurry, underbrush, and cream, this isn't the same night, or the same cold, as the metal fridges and men in white under fluorescent lights. This is endless nature, frost forming a pale crust, the morning fog weightless above the fields.

His first night is short, his slumber troubled beneath the eaves. The squeaky metal bed, the scratchy linen sheets, the frenetic if soft-footed patter of mice racing along the beams, the moon penetrating the thin curtains, the floor noisy as the hold of a ship out at sea, the sounds of the countryside, of life buzzing low to the ground and in the branches, an owl and a shrew, it'll take some getting used to.

At 6:00 a.m. it's a dry breakfast cookie dunked into a cup of coffee, radio tuned to the morning news, then work overalls are donned, followed by boots, a wool cap, and a fleece-lined jacket, and the breeder leads the way in the dark.

Pim follows, an invisible hand squeezing his heart, it's nerves, the emotion, the ambient calm, a thick silence interrupted only by the animals' heavy breathing, clouds of steam exhaled by nostrils gleaming in the dimness. It's time for the first milking: Pim is going to learn how to operate the milking machine, how to delicately attach the plastic cups to the cows' udders without hurting their teats soft as satin. Teats that aren't considered edible though they look appetizing enough with that soft pink hue. Pim the carnivore wouldn't mind taking a bite, he'd cut them into thin slices, he's imagining mammaries on display, but this kind of meat leaks milk not blood.

The breeder inspects one of his cow's painful horns. They grew askew and now they're pushing into the animal's head, just above the eyes, at the base of its forehead. He takes a sawing wire out of his pocket and attacks the horns with a vigorous back-and-forth movement. Pim holds the cow's head apprehensively (it's his first time handling the head of a living cow) as the breeder cuts. The pointy pieces detach, leaving raw flesh visible, the cows pulls away from Pim's grip.

The animals' heavy and aromatic smell warms the air. They're standing in straw up to their knees and outside it's thick mud, puddles, and fog. The breeder hands Pim a dung shovel, the manure fork, *You wanna avoid getting a tail smack to the face while you spread the straw. Tie the tail like this to the rear leg so it doesn't whip through the air.*

Dozens of round, muscled rumps that surely would be nice to pat are lined up in a row, heads lowered to the trough, an automated system that the cows can operate themselves, nudging the levers with their muzzles, nostrils dunked in the cool water, there's one that inhales a dozen liters in a few seconds without a dribble. Pim listens to them masticate, ruminate disinterestedly, regurgitate the prechewed hay stocked in their warm bellies, cows are nature-digesting machines, the fields have been torn apart and the milk is flowing, there's an aftertaste of peppery grass and soon, marbled meat. Pim is intoxicated by these smells that spread through him like liquor, he takes a deep breath, lulled by the continuous sounds of mastication and breathing, the noise of straw beneath impatient hooves, the comfortable grunts and lazy sighs made by these mammary-bearing creatures now flanked by the milking machine pumping and purring like a mechanical calf. Milky liquid spurts into the tube like blinding white blood, a reminder of the slaughtered pig, but everything is the color of snow, the color of clouds and whitewash. Pim wishes he could taste this liquid filling the vats, slurp up the creamy, pungent milk, feel it, heavy, descend through his body and coat his stomach with a layer of fatty foam. He feels full of affection for these creatures, these creatures swelling with meat, with the promise of abundance.

The night before, in the fluorescent-lit kitchen, the breeder warned Pim about sentimentality. *You can't get too attached to the animals, if you do you're screwed. They're not pets. It gets complicated because they're not things but they're not people either. If you develop feelings bout them it's too hard afterwards to send them to the slaughterhouse. I mean, you can be fond of a chicken, why not, it won't leave you heartbroken, but a cow? Of course the problem is that it's easier to get attached to a cow than to a hen.* Because there's a resemblance between cow and man—those deep black eyes fringed with lashes, watching us. It's the eyelashes that bring us closer, those long, curled lashes disconcert us and move us to tears.

A chicken's beady, lifeless eyes don't conjure up anything, nor are they watching us. Hens don't have eyelashes, their eyes are round and fixed, a moronic animal actually, have you seen how they walk? Plus their meat is white. No blood, no eyelashes, no sentimentality.

Snakes, flies, and moles don't have eyelashes and so we don't love them, we don't go near them, we don't pet them.

But Pim isn't afraid of affection, he's already showered plenty on his steaks.

Now he's alone with the cows, the breeder left him on his own so he can get acclimated. He stretches out in the fresh straw at the feet of a peaceful cow absorbed in her food, then pivots so he's between her two back hooves, his head the same direction as hers, he uses his legs to scoot himself underneath her swollen, disproportionate white belly—if the cow were to flop down Pim would be crushed, flattened. The cow's name is Culotte, she stands 1.5 meters at the withers and weighs 1,700 pounds. Her white coat is mottled with brown, notably around her eyes and mouth, her snout is short, her forehead wide and depressed between her eyes. Her fur is a little thicker at the neck and joints.

Beneath the cow like beneath the starry sky, hands clasped behind his head, chewing on a stalk of hay, Pim makes a mental list of the duties awaiting him: milk, currycomb the cows, clean their tails, rinse off the mud, tend to their feet, file their hooves, remove the crud. He might have to help the veterinarian on calving nights, pull on the calf, rub it with hay, feed it with a bottle. He'll have to take care of these creatures, keep them healthy, and extract as much calcium as possible from their underbellies. When everyone's done their job the cow will be sent to slaughter because she was born beef.

Culotte starts pissing noisily, the stream of urine splatters on Pim and interrupts his musings. He's on his hands and knees in the straw, still beneath the animal who with a silent, restrained kick gets rid of the intruder. Pim rolls onto his side, stands up, then the cow turns her head toward the butcher and watches him. Charcoal eyes, deep circles beneath, and eyelashes long as feathers.

Pim's never looked a cow in the eyes. He only knows the closed, pallid eyelids of a calf's head, its pupils frozen. He only knows cows in herds. You'll often spot them when driving down a country road. Grazing in a field, they turn toward you with their heavy heads and don't look away until you've vanished beyond the horizon. They always wait until you exit their field of vision before resuming the course of their ruminating lives.

Pim steps to the side, Culotte's eyes follow the movement, her massive, gleaming pupils fixed on Pim's like poisoned darts.

The breeder said it, you need to take the time to watch the animals, observe them, to learn of course but also for the pleasure, and the strangeness.

But this morning in the stable Pim's not watching the cow, it's the opposite. He's being watched, she has the upper hand, she's taken the power, and the motionless creature doesn't relent, she doesn't blink. Pim pivots slowly so he's opposite the cow, his back to the trough; now they're face to face. Intimidated and confused, he looks down then back up hoping the animal's moved on to something else, that she's found a new obsession, a new target, but their eyes meet again and it's a mix of surprise and unease.

You've got the one-up girl, you know I'm new here, you wanna test me is that it? Culotte remains silent, her nostrils quiver from the sustained effort of breathing, but nothing else moves. Tiny fluffy clouds float out of her gleaming muzzle; Pim matches the rhythm of his breathing to hers. If this is a duel Pim's victory is far from certain.

He closes his eyes, inhales, and focuses; he clenches his fists, sets his jaw, he becomes the sorcerer, the shaman, summons the animal spirits, he digs deep and imagines himself a cow. He mobilizes their shared DNA, his stomach curves and swells, his nose grows moist and puffy, his face flattens, his skin grows a short-haired coat, horns emerge, piercing through the skin on his forehead, his ears enlarge, Pim falls to all fours. The metamorphosis only lasts a moment and Pim regains human form when he reopens his eyes, the enigma of the cow still unsolved, as his epiphany fades.

The duel resumes, Pim tenses, his limbs stiff, but he doesn't dare move again. Culotte, inscrutable, maintains the pressure of her bottomless gaze. Hypotheses are whirling inside Pim's head, a thousand questions heating up his temples, while Culotte reads his mind. Culotte knows everything, sees everything. Cows have panoramic vision, or almost. Nothing gets by them, they know the earth is round, and you can't surprise them, they'll see you coming.

Cows have eyes in the back of their head and on either side, they sweep their surroundings; with those eyes the cow can see inside of Pim, top to bottom and diagonally, she looks him through and through, she sees Pim's disarray, the cow thinks it's funny to play with Pim's nerves this way, she sees his heart pounding furiously, his guts twitching, and the tears stockpiled behind his eyes, ready to gush.

Hang on, what are you looking at? It would appear that the cow has now dropped her gaze to the level of Pim's fly and is insistently staring at his crotch. His hand moves in a vague attempt at modesty. *You are a serious perv, cow. Are you checking me out?* Pim still can't decipher her look: mockery, surprise, accusation, who's to say?

What's going on inside that big head of yours, cow? What ideas are churning in that thick skull? Plans for a barn uprising? Escape? Vengeance? Or do you want to be my friend? I think that if you talked you would yell at me. All you're missing is speech but man are you missing it.

All you're missing is speech cow but boy are you missing it—Pim raised his voice, Culotte moved, finally, he has the upper hand again, she turns her head, annoyed, pouty, and plunges it back into her food, her refuge.

Pim backs out of the stable and takes a seat on a small milking stool forgotten at the entrance.

THE STORY OF THE KILLER PIG

The pig is foul-tempered, volatile, and violent. At birth he is the sole survivor of a litter of six. His mother, a sow gone mad, devours his five brothers and sisters before his eyes. He waits his turn, having given up on life all the more easily since he's only fleetingly acquainted with the opaque reality we call existence, but the sow doesn't want him. It's not that she's sparing him, rather that her disinterest and disdain for this piglet are such that she doesn't even consider him worthy of eating. The pig is off to a bad start.

The farmer, after killing the mother with a hammer blow to the back of the head, decides to keep the little pig and fatten him up.

One morning, while the now-grown pig is roaming the village streets in search of rubbish, a four-year-old boy happens by, the youngest son of a local wealthy family. The animal leaps onto the child, bites off his ears, and runs away. The young boy won't survive his injuries.

All the farmers in the village are mobilized, a search is conducted in the surrounding countryside, eventually the creature's prints are spotted along a muddy trail through the underbrush, he's tracked, he's found, and he's apprehended. The pig is tied up then transported to the village in a wheelbarrow. He's thrown in jail, everything done by the book, meaning straw, water, and bread.

A lawyer is appointed by the court. He has the difficult task of explaining the pig's barbaric act, of providing extenuating circumstances. Will the original infanticide be enough to obtain the judges' clemency? The animal's nasty temperament is no secret, he's known to be impulsive and mercurial. The owner, questioned, can only confirm that reputation.

The pig stays locked up for three weeks. He lives with the rats in the rancid dampness of his prison. His straw is never changed, the dry bread gives him heartburn, and scant daylight filters in through a dirty window. Three weeks, that's how long it takes to determine the pig's guilt.

The prosecutor visits him several times during his detention, hoping to extract a confession, but the pig remains stubbornly silent. Torture is attempted but it's no use. The burning pincers applied to either side of his head only elicit groans of pain.

The day of the trial, the entire village squeezes into the courtroom. The pig is waiting in the dock on all fours. He's wearing puffy, grayish trousers and a canvas jacket with holes. The prosecutor addresses the pig: *Stand up, pig! Everyone here is familiar with your brutish personality and uncivilized comportment. Sadly, this crime was predictable.*

What do you have to say in your defense? Obstinate silence from the pig, whose inaudible oinks aren't considered a valid reply.

As expected, the lawyer's arguments, invoking a difficult childhood marked by a lasting trauma, fail to convince.

The charges and conviction are read aloud: the homicidal pig is sentenced to death by hanging.

The execution will take place the following day and the entire village is invited to watch. Farmers are asked to come with their animals so the latter can be shown what awaits them if they were to commit a similar crime. The pig will be hanged as an example. At noon, the animal is brought to the scaffold. The owner, himself charged with paying damages to the family, is watching a major source of income vanish. Indeed, the pig was supposed to be slaughtered and sold.

Dressed in the same questionable suit he wore during his trial, the reviled creature is presented to the crowd. The hangman first slices off his snout with a sudden ax blow then slips a mask with a human face on him. Next the pig is hanged by the neck. But his thick layers of muscle and fat protect him from choking and the rope slides down this armor of flesh. Finally the animal is suspended by his rear hooves, stunned, and his throat is slit. The crowd applauds wildly, hats fly. The few pigs present, pallid and shocked, cast distressed looks at their indifferent owners, while the hens, horses, and rabbits discreetly avert their gaze.

On the farm the days pass and they are whole seasons—rain, pink sky, clouds stretching across the horizon, a dampened sun and supple woodland, blinding green—the days go by organized around milkings, and the repetition of tasks— stable to clean, fodder to distribute—isn't monotonous but gentle and comforting. Pim works diligently, as devoted to his job as a cowherd as he is to that of a butcher. Pim takes on every role, he's amenable and adaptable, everything suits him, everything pleases him, everything lights a fire inside him, put a tool in his hands, a boning knife or a pitchfork, and just look at that passion, that jubilation, there's madness there but it's contained, muted, betrayed only by the galvanizing repetition of his movements. Pim is an opaque young man, a calm sea, Pim is a man of action, the sum total of his movements. If anything surges from the depths it's tears and nothing else. If anything overflows, bursts, transforms his face, it's those unreadable but undeniable tears.

He gets used to his bedroom beneath the squeaking beams, collapses there at night, exhausted and at peace, sleeps like a log until the first milking at dawn. Pim and the breeder cohabit their respective silences, their shared labor, and their mutual trust. Meals are eaten together on the long, narrow table, they discuss the health of the herd, the color of the sky, the grain crisis, veterinary costs or European standards, sometimes their voices drown out the nightly news broadcast from an old television on the sideboard.

Dinner is followed by a silent digestive walk, contemplation of the Big Dipper, the sour, stubborn taste of apple liquor in their mouths.

Pim focuses all his attention on the cows the way he does on meat to be carved, Pim only does one thing at a time, a single thing with his life and today it's the cows demanding his time and devotion, today nothing else is more important than these creatures, today he sinks joyfully into the existence of others, animals though they may be.

Culotte especially, the favorite, the chosen one, his former inquisitor and now friend. When Pim enters the stable, he calls her first, she rises, recognizes him, speaks to him. She makes noises, exhales, lows, scratches, she says things that sound like contentment, that take the form of high-pitched, drawling sounds. Pim comes closer, the cow sniffs his clothes then his face, her large head pressed against Pim's angular features, her breath smelling of hay. Pim closes his eyes, enjoys the moment, waits for the vigorous lick, the thick, rough tongue that goes up from chin to forehead then down, forehead to chin. Pim holds out his hand, Culotte moves back slightly, lies down in her stall, he sits beside her, strokes her head, rubs the hair behind her ear, she lets him, her petrol-colored eyes still fixed on Pim's but this time without animosity. The occupant of the neighboring stall watches them then looks away, almost like she's waiting for the show of intimacy to conclude. Pim places Culotte's head in the crook of his arms, gently pulls her toward him, now he places his head against the cow's forehead, this time he hugs her, caresses the warm, coarse coat of her cheek, this goes on for a bit, he's thinking about meat.

Before Culotte goes out to the pasture, returns to the open air and the green earth, the fresh backdrop of the countryside— she'll be spotted in the distance, children will press against car windows to excitedly point her out—Pim gets her ready: he currycombs her coat hardened by barn living, meticulously rubs her horns with an oiled rag and scrapes off mud residue so they shine like the tusks of a white elephant bathed in the waters of the Ganges. He'd have liked to hang glass beads from her ears, place a gold ring through her nostrils, would have liked to tattoo mystical patterns on her flanks, colorful arabesques between her eyes. He scrubs the dirt off her tail and hooves then shears the cow, starts with the feet, moves up to the stomach, the back, along the spinal column then around the base of the tail, and finally, very delicately, he shears around the teats. There's some pilling on the belly, but now her coat is short and homogenous. Tears roll down only to disappear inside the furrows along his cheeks, Pim stopped wiping them away a long time ago, otherwise he'd never see the end of it, he waits for them to dry, to evaporate, for the skin to prickle and pull. Pim gets tears the way you inhale pollen in the early days of spring: his eyes sting, crisscross with tiny red vessels, these burst and trickle, liquid explosions, pupils like erupting volcanoes. He contemplates the cow, her head, her eyes, her nose, her nostrils, then her powerful, curved body, the dark spots on a white coat, the thick warmth, he touches her, her stomach filled with a mash of chewed grass. Every element of the cow is peaceful, everything is slow, every stage of her simultaneously economical and productive metabolism appears calculated, a patient and weighty existence. The life of a cow is most often a still one, a life of restraint: the cow waits, available and placid, then suddenly deflates like a punctured goatskin and this yields yogurt and later roast beef. What does it mean to be a cow? Nothing if not the seasons, food, a man's hand on her teats and on her throat.

If you were to open up a cow's flat skull, if Pim were to delicately trepan it with a wire butter slicer and then slip inside the cranium, squeezing between the brain and the eye, here's what he would see, lodged behind the creature's pupil, his man's eye pressed against the cow's: he would have a view of the world, he would be able to watch his peers through a bovine eye that curves reality, he would see only their movements, their gaits, human existences through a sieve, he would hear only their intonations, smell only their odors, he would sense their kindness or brutality. Pim would see only shapes—breeders, dairy farmers, cowherds, veterinarians, and market vendors hoping to make their fortune. And beyond those silhouettes, melting into the horizon, he would see the starving, bleating masses that need to be fed. Pim saw what the cow sees, maybe Pim is an angel who speaks to Norman cattle, a saint who blesses meat, a sorcerer of butchery, or a visionary of the pastures. He visits the honeycombs of time, he remembers drawing a cow on a cave wall with the blood of the sacrificed animal, he remembers that it was sacred and immolated, prayed for, venerated, and transformed into gold. He remembers domesticating it, sawing off its horns and nailing them above the hearth, butchering the animal to make a cloak from its hide, marking it with red iron, and, finally, roasting it over the fire. You are an endearing creature, cow, you served me well and now you know who I am.

You have to like animals, not necessarily domesticated ones, cats and dogs, not wild animals either, hyenas or lions, but familiar animals, the tamed and profitable ones. Pim already knows he'll die like an animal, he knows that when it's time to go he'll join the hogs in their muck. People rarely know how to die but animals do, it suffices to observe them and mirror what they do. They find a spot, a little corner, and they wait discreetly, they control their breathing, count down the minutes, sometimes the hours, try not to be a bother, not to attract much notice, they don't make a sound. Animals are exemplary when it comes to dying but they don't know that.

You have to like the animals that teach us how to die because we're all going to die the same death, no one will be spared, animals tell us there's no way out, for them like for us, we're all corpses in the end. They also teach us how to live, in excess, since beasts are man's fever: we will suffer just like them, we're large cuts of raw beef, our bodies escape us, slip between our fingers, slip out of our awareness.

The breeder is listening at the barn door, he's listening to Pim talk to the animals. All breeders talk to their cows, but with Pim it's different, he's making conversation with the cow, he doesn't merely give orders, reassurance, congratulations, or encouragement, he includes himself, he says us, he says you and me, he goes far indeed, he walks toward the cow, opens his arms wide, as wide as the Messiah on the cross, he says *Our fates are linked yours and mine, I'm going to carve you up*

*with care and respect, you'll be well treated you'll see because I'm
butcher-man and I have the power.*

He methodically strokes the animal, his hand goes all
over the cow, blood pounding in her veins, veins that course
beneath a vast pelt, beneath flesh he imagines, Pim makes
his way across the animal's body like the body of the girl in
his bed, cheek first then the neck, the chuck, he descends
toward the brisket, the shank, back up toward the rib and
short loin, and down again toward the short plate, then
along the sirloin—bottom sirloin, top sirloin, tenderloin—
his hand completes its journey at the cow's hindquarters—
rump roast.

The contact between their two bodies, his palm on her
flank, sends shivers through him, a prickling in his lower
stomach, his legs are wobbly, head spinning, senses spinning, more tears, this time they fall onto the animal's coat,
absorbed by hairs like Gore-Tex fabric, but the cow doesn't
feel anything, she's grazing indifferently, it would take a
waterfall of tears over her head to get a reaction.

After one month on the farm, in the fresh air, Pim has
acquired a tan, his arms are slightly thicker, his chest has
filled out from the accumulated effect of physical labor—
buckets to carry, hay to sweep, coats to comb, it's nonstop,
shovel and pitchfork.

After one month on the farm, Pim has seen animals of the field, observed their rumen swell and get covered with fat, their bright, promising eyes. He's inhaled the fertile pasture smell that seeps into the folds of muscles and softens the nerves.

Pim made his return to the animal kingdom but now it's time to double back, to take a running start along the meat chain, to swap the barn for the cold room, to take his place again at the end of the line.

Mention in the local edition of *Ouest-France*, a quarter page. A black and white photo shows Pim in profile, visibly anxious, leaning over a piece of beef, knife primed to carve. The caption reads: "Pim of Ploufragan, best apprentice butcher in Côtes-d'Armor."

The cutting room of the Sanzot butchery in Paimpol was transformed on Wednesday into an exam room. Five young trainees competed for the title of Best Apprentice Butcher in Côtes-d'Armor. The candidates had three hours to prepare a leg of beef, a lamb shoulder, and a veal shoulder. The examiner was none other than Léandre Le Tallec, treasurer of the butchers' union and himself a butcher in Paimpol. "What we're judging here is the skillful execution of boning and dressing techniques, as well as the handling and presentation of the final product," explained Léandre Le Tallec, who noted that artisanal professions undervalued for many years are making a comeback.

After winning the title of best apprentice butcher in Côtes-d'Armor, Pim will participate in the Brittany regional championship in Bruz, outside of Rennes. If he finishes in one of the top four spots, in June he'll be heading to nationals in the Eure.

II

He traveled, he left Brittany.

He came to know the wholesalers' melancholy in the early hours, the cold wake-up call of the meat locker, the intoxication of the job and the cleaver, the bitterness of blood that tastes of mercury.

He opened his butcher shop in Paris.

One of the world's best meat cities, where presentation is an art and a calling, where the standard cut (far more delicate and finely crafted than your basic Breton cut) requires the utmost skill.

Pim came to Paris a stubborn, solitary, and meticulous man.

That's all there is. Butchery hasn't left room for anything else; it's bled into an otherwise empty life, family and few friends forgotten, the rare female companion, the rare distraction, an inordinate zeal for the job, a frenzied joy, a vocation, an exacting obsession. Pim the butcher-soldier galvanized by all the hours put in. He's thriving, the money's coming in and piling up in a corner of his life, a life that's nothing more than the time given us.

Pim devotes himself exclusively to the continuous improvement of his craft and his expertise, and he knows what he's talking about. Invited regularly to speak at conferences on the future of the Norman cow, the capacities of the Bresse chicken, or the butchery potential of grass-fed cattle, Pim is reputed for his excellent communication skills and his informed and passionate lectures. He studies the Blonde d'Aquitaine's short-haired coat and the delicate fibers of its meat, he pontificates about the paleness of the Charolais, and the generous redheaded Limousin, he pays homage to the western white pig and its high-quality fat, to the black-rumped Limousin pig with its large kidneys and small forward-pointing ears, to the famous Miélan pig and its round, raised ribs, whose ability to be fattened is remarkable and who produces firm and savory lard. He's fond of these devoted, edible beasts, he admires their gustatory power and their sense of sacrifice. *We owe them a lot, namely our good health and our survival. Animals know that nature does nothing in vain, in a void, they know their own utility and their purpose, to serve us, cannon fodder for the human race*, clap clap clap.

On the sign overhanging the storefront, painted in gold letters, it reads: PIM'S BUTCHER SHOP.

Inside, the window display is arranged by meat and by color, the cuts gleaming like diamond necklaces. For fifteen feet, the eye goes from reddest—vermilion beef and scarlet lamb—to lightest—pinkish or translucent veal, poultry, wan pork. At the end, where the counter curves, sit the rillettes, chipolata, and dry-cured hams, all embellished with decorative plastic greenery. There are a few hanging chickens, their miserable little necks stretching toward the ceiling, their flabby, goose-pimpled skin trimmed with tricolored ribbon.

A grinder placed on the edge of the butcher block makes a dull noise as meat emerges in long limber threads before landing on a sheet of wax paper.

On the floor footprints are preserved in a thin carpet of sawdust. The wood powder absorbs the speckles of fat dispersed by the butcher's saw: a thin fog of meat particles that hangs in the air then falls like a cloud of dew.

On the wall across from the display, dark wooden shelves are lined with canned flageolet beans, instant mashed potatoes, chips, jars of Béarnaise sauce, country pâté, and bottles of local wine. A fluorescent blue light captures and toasts flies; upon landing, the insects' wings burn with a delicious crackle.

On the wall, medals, plaques, and slates boasting authenticity, traceability, and protected designation of origin. Three framed cow portraits are the only decorative elements: a Salers, an Aubrac, and a Charolais. They stare into the camera, heavy bells of engraved bronze around their necks, sparkling pastures in the background.

This morning, Pim is being delivered 5,000 euros worth of beef, quarter- or half-carcasses. It's 7:00 a.m., the butcher is looking out for the truck, impatient to see the meat, to feel it in his palm and in his heart, one deep breath and that fresh smell spreading through his chest, he's impatient to tenderly remove the skin, to peel the thin white film off dented muscle, to reveal the deep, smooth redness, to place his blade on the mass before him and reduce it to round slices, to dramatically whet his knife, whet it so finely he could split an eyelash.

The truck's here and men wearing smocks beneath their large white cowls, monks of meat, carry the merchandise on their backs, breathing heavily.

Pim watches the procession of meat arrive. Inside the butcher's mind germinates the absurd and dubious idea to undress, to roll around buck naked in the meat like in waves white with foam or a field of thick grass. He could lock himself inside the cold room, take off his clothes, sidle up to the bacon, and rub. His warm dry body transmitting a little heat to the cold meat or vice versa. But there's the matter of hygiene, which can't be compromised, you never take the risk of contaminating the meat through a nagging cough or a cold sore.

It's important to have a good butcher, the older you get the more importance they take on in our lives, if you can afford meat that is. You hope for the butcher's best cuts, the pieces they fetch from the back.

Pim's butcher shop opens at 7:30 but there's always a few people drumming on the metal roll-up door ahead of time, impatient and straight from bed, there's always a few who count on their daily dose of ground beef down to the gram, a few who want to see the whole animal before buying a pork chop, who demand to visit the cold room, to check the health certificates. There's a few who are bothered by the sound of the knife like nails on a chalkboard, they leave the shop gritting their teeth, with a pained, reproachful grimace, there's a few who want you to set something aside for them, who buy the best cuts for their cat, who ask if they can pick up the bones tonight at closing.

There's one customer who buys a fresh calf brain every Friday. Pim stocks up on brains solely for this sinewy young woman with ash-blonde hair. Because nobody buys offal anymore, people want prepared dishes, want it quick, pre-cooked, but this unique individual is attached to her weekly brain, gray matter served in sauce, so she can stay in shape, senses alert, mental calculations honed. She believes in the transfer of neurons. Eat brains and you'll get smarter, my girl. But is the veal a clever animal? Mightn't she risk mental degeneration? When I eat steak the blood enters my blood, so if I eat brains why wouldn't it enter my brain?

And inside the calf's brain is its whole life, its short, juvenile life, a black box of sorts that contains its retinal afterimages and its fears, colors, seasons, the taste of a meadow and of a mother. We're eating imprinted matter, encoded matter and you won't convince me that it's harmless, nobody eats brain anymore, ask yourself why that is. It's not a question of trends, it's that we realized the effects in the end, that there were irreversible transfers. Eat calf brain and you become a calf (rediscovering, for example, the flavors of milk). It's different for the other organs, they don't have consequences on your soul. If you need proof look no further than the fact that we have a brain, a liver, and feet, like animals, but no flank steak, no London broil, you can't deny the obvious conclusions.

You have kind of an odd profession, Mr. Pim, you expose us to radioactive animals, our bodies mingle, I can feel it when I swallow my steak, something quivers as the meat goes down, then slowly fades. It's the wild beast entering me. My body has the enzyme that digests elastin, and I can remember the first meat I ever ate. I was still perched in my high chair when I spat chewed-up beef at my dad's head. The first meat I ever ate sealed my dependency on animals, I caught it like a virus. I eat and I am a carnivorous creature, a common weasel, a brown bear, a lion of the Kalahari.

Incidentally meat is in style: bacon neckties, 100% wool bedspreads in the shape of a prime rib, steak motif wallpaper—raw is back, baby, art exhibitions set up like cold rooms, models photographed leaning sensually against animal carcasses, the First Lady of France at the famous Rungis wholesale market, meat is à la mode this season. Lady Gaga the kooky butcher comes to us live from Los Angeles at the MTV Music Awards. The singer goes onstage in an outfit made entirely of raw meat, two thousand dollars' worth of chuck on her back and quite the smell: a low-cut beef minidress accessorized with a diamond necklace and fishnet stockings, an angled fascinator atop platinum blonde hair—it's a tournedos in fact—a handbag made of fresh meat and sirloin platform shoes. The ensemble is scandalous. Only a woman would do such a thing. Because women know that we're just meat, they know it better than anyone.

Women and Pim the butcher, who placed a framed photo of Lady Gaga in her meat dress beside his cows. Posters of naked women in trucker cabs, a pop star draped in steaks above the cash register.

On Tuesdays Pim goes to Rungis and every week it's a joy to climb into his white minivan in the early hours, a joy intensified in winter when the frost settles and the air is biting. It's 4:00 a.m. and Pim is driving to the largest fresh produce market in Europe as the slaughterhouse trucks are departing, merchandise unloaded. At 4:00 a.m. cuts are still being refined, meat carved into ever smaller pieces, entire carcasses chopped to fit inside utility vehicles, inside Pim's Peugeot, whose chiller box can hold up to 1,500 pounds of meat.

At 4:30 a.m. the first traffic jams form at the Rungis access points, vehicles wait patiently in line, slowed down by customs checks, then the massive site fills the skyline, warehouses as far as the eye can see, the trail of trucks beneath streetlamps' weak halos, old Renault Estafette vans, refrigerated cars, and forklifts. Twenty bistros, erected between the warehouses, bustle twenty-four hours a day, people come from Paris before the sun has even risen for a rib eye that travels less than a hundred feet to reach the plate, served rare with maître d'hôtel butter and steak fries; performers and wholesale meat traders sit side by side on booth seats, it's a black-and-white film, the pinball machine's out of order and the house wine costs 1.50 euros a glass.

Pim drives past the auction house, the flower pavilions, the fruit and vegetable sector hemmed in by a ring of cold and whose never-ending aisles are navigated by bicycle. He parks in front of the tripe vendors, beside a black Porsche, stops at the public urinal reeking of ammonia and piss, crying as he urinates—this morning it's tiny room-temperature tears—throws on a coat with an embroidered label MEAT MADE IN FRANCE and his hat, rinses his hands at one of the outside fountains, enters the tripe hall, section five.

Pim shops exclusively at Prodal (the first stall on the left when you enter). That's where he finds his only friends, only acquaintances rather, a world of men whose rough camaraderie is forged in the cold and in the dark, men in white stained with blood, bundled up in thick fleeces beneath their coats, affable, cheerful men quick to make a sale.

Pim inspects lamb and veal sweetbreads, assesses their delicate texture, and anticipates their flavor. A merchant places two large white glands taken from a young animal's throat in his hand. They're nice and firm, pearly white with a pink undertone, puffy and wet, they're perfect. Next Pim considers lamb testicles, veined with blue and sold in bags of thirty, and hesitates. There are livers too, magnificent, enormous livers, like scarlet jellyfish. They drip, stacked on shelves, shining like vinyl, soft and smooth, you can see your reflection. Calf or heifer livers, pink or garnet-colored, alongside purple-velvet kidneys tossed haphazardly into plastic yellow bins, buckets of pork meatballs beneath hanging giblets, and the meat is so tender and unmarred it's like their hearts are still beating. Pim wishes he could buy everything, own everything, embrace everything, all those delicate textures, those endless hues of red, the tongues lined up on hooks, the pork cheeks, the mounds of lamb feet (though who still eats *pieds paquets*, a mixture of feet and tripe that needs to simmer for at least eight hours before it can be consumed?). A cow's stomach reposes in a bucket, honeycomb and reed tripe, a patchy blanket speckled with tiny rubbery cavities. At the end of the warehouse, calf heads hang on hooks, lined up by the dozens, a soft and romantic shade of pink. Their skin is wrinkled around half-shut eyes, offering a glimpse of sneering indigo-blue pupils. A constellation of red dots around the eyebrows and snouts, foreheads marked by a scarlet perforation.

At 5:30 Pim leaves the tripe hall for the main meat pavilion, he'll visit every section, veal, beef, mutton, but he'll start with pork. A miniature pork assembly line is working in high gear to process 600 animals before dawn. On either side of a conveyor belt a dozen workers chop up the half-carcasses in rhythm, four minutes per animal, one takes the hooves, another the ears, the head, the hock, the animal makes its way down the belt, reduced to pieces, unrecognizable by the end of the line. The noise of electric saws drowns out the clamor of buying and selling. Pim's looking to purchase a leg of ham at the best price, a large rump sliced at the hip joints.

The meat pavilion is the biggest of them all. Along a central aisle six hundred feet long, carcasses stretch as far as the eye can see, lined up like in a vast refrigerated parking lot. The ceiling is crisscrossed by movable rails from which meat hangs in clusters. Hundreds of men conduct business beside labeled half-cows and shelves of prime rib. They circulate amid this massive spread of muscle, slide carcasses along the rails, maneuver mechanical arms on the truck loading dock. Warehouse workers push shopping carts to utility vehicles, they carry boxes and skinned animals on their shoulders.

Pim weaves, he zigzags, at the center of this hurrying industrious swarm, he casts quick and knowledgeable glances at the merchandise, a look of disdain for the carcasses whose bones are too thin, the ones disguised as bodybuilder cows with pronounced rumps, glistening specimens with perfectly sculpted muscles but whose meat is flavorless and water-bloated, industrial dairy cows that churn out milk their whole lives then end up at the slaughterhouse, that tired old meat that sustains us—fast food, microwave dinners, and supermarkets. Pim, ever demanding, ever refined, ever obsessive, doesn't want to hear about cull cows slaughtered at the age of two, about cattle fattened up in 200 days with corn sludge and beet pulp, a high-protein diet composed of growth hormones and antibiotics. He demands the grass-fed cow who's grazed at pasture, a proper animal that reached maturity by taking its time, fat and sun-basked, he wants green fields in the heights of the Aubrac, lush grass at an altitude of 300 feet, he imagines himself in a hemp coat and hardy boots making his way through the meat market in the village square, haggling over a prizewinning animal worth 3,000 euros and clocking in at 1,000 pounds, a hand on his shoulder and a shot of bitter Salers, he pictures himself going up the small rocky path that leads to the breeder, the breeder who finished his cow the old-fashioned way and is now watching the departure of the creature he brought into this world with a pang in his heart—*she gave me seven calves in four years sweet little thing.*

Pim wants cows that have been cared for. Pim, who saw a report on TV, wants Japanese cattle raised in Spain in an idyllic setting. Onscreen: happy creatures (happiness assured by a voice-over) with silky coats and majestic rumps, turning their gleaming gaze toward the camera, placidly ruminating, red wine and fresh grain on tap. Organic only and locally produced on the farm. The wine—some people drink Actimel and weigh 130 pounds; these cows get a liter of wine per day, first thing in the morning, and weigh one ton—is for extra energy. The grain is meticulously prepared, like for a newborn or the elderly: triple-washed, cooked, ground for better digestion. The hay beds are changed every week to prevent foul odors. There are 1,500 cows and each one is milked individually, with the utmost attention.

But what makes their meat particularly tender isn't the food or the alcohol, it's the music. Music softens the beef, especially classical music, and Verdi more than Wagner. So the cows eat to music, drink to music, and shit to music, thanks to the multiple speakers scattered throughout the beatific barn and connected to the turntable of a local DJ passionate about chamber music. All that comfort ensures that fat penetrates the fibers and produces premium marbled meat. And steaks at double the price.

A kilo of beef raised on vino and Vivaldi: 6 euros. A kilo of industrial beef: 2.50 euros.

2.50 euros for a well-padded animal stuffed with steroids, who fattens up twice as fast. Or 2.50 euros for a Brazilian zebu raised on a vast genetically modified prairie, on fluorescent green grass capable of hosting twice as much cattle (zebus are easy to bone, the carving is quick, the meat is tender, no fat, no taste either, but it'll dominate the market you'll see, it will dethrone our dairy cows, because Brazil is more than just soccer and G-strings).

Maybe Pim will eventually come to terms with it, just like he'll come to terms with chickens raised in forty days in the dark and whose legs can't support them, just like he'll come to terms with three Breton hogs per square yard of slatted flooring.

Except if the carnivores retreat, if the vegetarians gain ground, if there are more and more consumers who see the cow on their plate, not a nice rare steak but a cow who stares them straight in the eyes, a look laden with reproach and woe, a look they'll take to the grave, that will follow them like a curse. The cow on the plate, popping up amid the fries, scrutinizing them, accusing them. Mr. and Mrs. leap out of their chairs and without a word, blindly tossing a fifty-euro bill onto the checkered tablecloth, leave the restaurant at a run—they won't be back.

The vegetarians will need to win the battle, but they're off to a rocky start seeing how the earth is swelling and demands to be fed, seeing how those too long nourished on dry bread and water wouldn't mind, it's only fair, a decent rib roast.

And so experts worry, scientists experiment, specialists sound the alarm, and butchers are invited to conferences about the future of butchery, the future of the carnivorous diet, the new meat of tomorrow. *Ladies and gentlemen, esteemed colleagues, we need to anticipate shortages, prevent the coming crisis, innovate and explore, the reign of French Limousin beef is over!*

At the last World Butchers conference Pim participated in a workshop dedicated to synthetic meat produced in test tubes. Meat grown by men and women in white coats with no bloodstains. Also under discussion was frog steak made from biopsies: you grow frog skeletal muscle, you remove cells, and you make steak. Unconvinced by the quality of this in-vitro meat, Pim then signed up for a presentation on organic meat made from insects—Dutch mealworms, Beninese beetles, and Laotian crickets.

The advantage of cricket over cow is that it doesn't take up much space, doesn't fart, doesn't emit eighteen times its weight in carbon dioxide, doesn't create inconsiderate holes in the ozone layer. Still, it does produce meat that crunches in your mouth and that some might find unpleasant. The Beninese beetle, however, is less crunchy and can be found by the millions in tree trunks, you simply grab your dugout canoe, go deep into the forest, have at it with a machete. The Beninese beetle counts just as much as a steak, it even counts double a chicken since it contains 40% protein versus 20% for poultry. We'll eat them pan-fried, at first our forks will wobble, we'll close our eyes, disgusted by the consistency, then we'll dive in and we'll get used to it just fine, the way we do everything, to kiwis in the 1970s, the euro in 2000. In fifty years, Laotian insect farming will feed the planet.

A documentary shown at the end of the presentation is meant to leave participants convinced. It shows a butcher from Limoges riding in a rickshaw along the Mekong River, heading toward a farm belonging to Yupa Dee, his supplier. The air is heavy, the sky whitewashed, the butcher mops his forehead repeatedly. Yupa's insect farm is at the end of a long road of burning asphalt. The breeder has a hundred cement cylinders in which he raises his domestic crickets, as well as red weevils and some weaver ants. He has the butcher taste his latest harvest, fried or boiled, with a side of rice. A good dose of calcium, seven times more than in the same quantity of beef, a caramelized and spicy taste, the butcher orders 600 pounds.

This is the future of butchery: insects and toads cooked BBQ-style, in a stew, or on a plancha. Pim is wary and in the meantime, until the future becomes the present, that's always how it goes, Pim wants to keep mining for gold, to be a humanist of meat, he wants to do a meticulous job using premium, irreproachable products.

Without a second glance he walks by displays of vacuum-packed meat, inferior quality, cheap restaurant fare, old leather hides cut into strips to look the part, animals boned for lazy butchers who have neither the know-how nor the time to cut their own meat. Before ending up as *steak-frites* at some train station bistro, these cows churned out Président brand Camembert for years, udders swollen like balloons.

Pim wants only the best carcasses, sold whole because real beauty doesn't need to hide, it flaunts itself top to bottom.

The butcher ignores the bad beef covered in fat, the meager carcasses, the thin, flat quarters. He searches for and eventually finds meat full of contrasts, a thin film of yellow fat intermingled with muscle, the latter hued pink, then dark purple, crimson on the thighs, and finally garnet on the rump. An animal veined in every shade of red like Rance marble, and speckled like the Veronese variety. He strokes the meat between the ribs—silk—then the protruding rib cage, the bulging hindquarters, the rounded muscles.

What Pim likes at Rungis is less this world of active men and more that of animals on hooks. He takes his time, annoyed by the persistent presence of the registered vendors, their incessant prattling, their hands heavy on his shoulder, their eyes gauging the carcass at the same time as his. He wishes they'd leave him alone, a little privacy with the meat before negotiating the price. But at Rungis everything is open, everything is visible, you can't go hide somewhere with your beef shank, you can't creep into a corner to empty out calf heads and then toss the skulls into the air the way you'd throw your hat into the sky in a burst of jubilation.

Pim spreads ribs, assesses their thickness, hand deep inside the animal, down to the elbow, makes sure the muscles are pale. Pim concludes his inspection with a careful reading of the identification card, kneels, for a few seconds he observes the fresh blood that's dripped beneath the carcass, staining the cement. He wipes the spot with the tip of his index finger, brings it to his mouth, closes his eyes. Pim, not a religious man except that meat is a religion, prays for silence, for this hangar echoing like a snare drum to empty of nonbelievers—a moment of grace. He stands up, *I'll take four lambs, that'll last me three days*, then hesitates in front of an eviscerated suckling pig, its belly skin hanging piteously.

At the market exit, large trash bags from the cutting stations overflow with chitlins, bits of fat, and dry, blackened scraps. At the sight of the leavings, Pim remembers a man telling him about the time he ate sheep fat in Kyrgyzstan: the fat cools immediately in your mouth, turns bitter, and is very difficult to chew.

A few figures creep by and they're not wearing the white regulatory garments; these furtive and hunched-over shadows hurriedly collect the meat leftovers, stuffing them into backpacks, shopping bags, baskets, or threadbare pockets, for resale to certain Chinese restaurants. Sometimes a merchant will catch one in the act by the coat collar, sometimes it's a child they let go with a smack to the back of the neck and a sigh of resignation. This large parallel operation of rubbish and recyclables, a harmless black market, is tiny when compared to the vastness of the never-ending bustle of Rungis. Pim doesn't want to see it, he averts his gaze.

On Tuesdays and Thursdays, when the dump truck goes round to all the butcher shops to collect fat, lard, and bones to be incinerated on the outskirts of town, Pim doesn't put out everything he has. He sets some aside, which he later tosses into the green bin outside his store. He knows that in a few hours, foragers will come pick up the scraps of meat that will be cooked over a rustic fire.

If you were to fall, Pim, and if your fall was far, would you become the butcher of sad scraps? Do you love meat enough to dig it out of a trash can and run it under clean water, cook it for hours until it's safe for consumption, dressed up in an envelope of heavily seasoned pastry dough? Meat is a treasure, a treasure that belongs to animals and gets taken by man. People would kill for a piece of meat, and in fact they do. People would eat another person for a piece of meat, and in fact they have.

It's 8:00 a.m., there's still haggling in the poultry hall, Pim navigates around pallets and stacks of cardboard boxes, around silky rabbits with their feet bound, dressed Bresse chickens, Vosges quails, feathered chickens tied with pink ribbon, guinea fowl and pheasants. The collective clamor of buyers and sellers rises beneath the glass ceiling like a cloud, it's time for the final sales, solace at the bar is imminent. Pim makes his way across the length of the hall to Saint Hubert, a bistro inside the marché, a heat bubble, where everyone finds themselves come morning: you remove the many layers of fleece wool under your coat, take off your hat, join the crowd at the zinc bar, now you're cornered. These men are dirty and exhausted, their faces red with broken blood vessels, cheeks violet, eyes seeping fatigue, noses streaked with veins, their energy is fading, and then the first round comes—*fill 'er up*. The windows turn opaque from the condensation, meanwhile inside the conversation turns to sales made, questions about the family, kids doing well in school? wife in good health? and complaints about restaurateurs: *Just watch 'em carve a flank steak, any which way, they don't deserve any better than the last of the rump to make their hamburgers, their nasty little steak tartares. Or hang on, how 'bout the eye round? They can have that too, vacuum-packed, nice and bloody, ready to be sliced and made into the all-you-can-eat carpaccio that's all the rage at Bistro Romain. Slice it thin and it's fine, but try for a beef roast and don't even get me started—totally inedible.*

Pim has always refused to eat the meat at Bistro Romain the same way he's always avoided kebabs, *meat scrap heaps*, as he calls them. Pim has never felt the late-night consolation of spit-roasted meat, never inhaled the greasy smell of veal, turkey, and chicken cut into thin strips and sitting in a pile.

Here it's a tripe sandwich and, someone else gets this round, a blackcurrant kir. Pim, who has already drunk five glasses, hasn't yet felt the fatigue hit him like a hailstorm, alcohol is keeping the exhaustion at bay, he's enjoying the momentary lethargy, stretches it out a bit longer, seated apart from the others, butchers' kinship notwithstanding, observing his peers benevolently, with affection.

A traveling salesman unrolls his felt mat on top of the counter, unzips his rolling suitcase, and sets out musical lighters, retractable pens, flashing badges, and pocket calculators.

By 9:00 a.m. the sun is up, Pim's cue to go back through the cold and now nearly deserted market, to feel the alcohol pounding at his temples and warming his legs, to push a cart of merchandise wrapped in tarps, to load the van and head back to the shop, a mountain of meat to cut.

Pim stops for tulips at the flower pavilion, he likes the dark ones, deep burgundy. He has his vendor, the one he trades with: a roast beef for a couple bunches of tulips. At Rungis meat is bartered for flowers.

Over time the butcher's skin mottles with red dots, the epidermis along his cheekbones flushed, his nose dappled with pale blood, his mucous membranes and lungs blotched with emanations of meat. Pim inhales these smells of rawness all year long, they wallpaper his body like red nicotine. Day after day, he breathes in these airborne living particles, which then inflate his own red blood cells, he gains in strength, he doesn't need to eat the meat, he breathes and digests it straight from the source, sometimes his nose bleeds: runoff.

Over time the butcher's hands swell and grow rounder, nails, knuckles, and veins disappearing into thickening flesh. His hands begin to resemble the meat they're manipulating, meathands indistinguishable from the roast being trussed at the speed of light.

Over time Pim is able to recognize every cut, eyes shut, but also eyes open, by color: a garnet tournedos, a carmine cheek, a scarlet flank steak. But by touch he's more confident still. He palpates, strokes, and kneads, he follows the movement and trajectory of the veins, presses the pad of his finger, his flesh, into the flesh of the meat; sirloin and skirt steaks are long meats, easy enough. Everything above the ribs, however, produces tighter cuts. Rib steak is thin and tri-tips, conical. The Parisian round is harder to identify in the dark but Pim always gets it right, there are two parts, one round and one flat, with a nerve in the middle. The finer and smoother the grain, without any checkered marks, the more delicious the meat. Limousin beef, for example: fine-grained, fine-boned.

If there were competitions, Pim would win them all. He would defeat any and all butchers wearing blindfolds. Cloth over his eyes, an audience energized by warm-up acts hired by the butchers' union, first prize of 10,000 euros plus a certificate on parchment paper, special recognition in gilded letters.

Pim is impermeable to brutality, a man without bile—a sour taste in your mouth, animal provenance or otherwise— despite the tragedy of butchery. Seen from the inside, inside Pim the butcher, everything appears joyful, a tangible and unadulterated sentiment, the joy of being consumed by one's work, a bonfire of joy, he started and he won't stop, he'll die onstage, it's habit now, hyperbolic motion, and soon the boomerang effect. The reasons behind this passion are hopelessly entangled, his motivations nothing compared to his actions, actions are what remain, what carve out existence, they are what accumulate, settle at the bottom, make a life.

Pim is off-center, a man who doesn't play the leading role in his own play, who occupies the back seat in this existence that's his all the same. Meat has the starring role.

Late morning. Back from Rungis, Pim is alone and silent before his butcher block. Hands nice and flat on the dented wood like two beef escalopes. He talks to his meat the way a breeder talks to his animals.

He's hunched over, his hand strokes the block, the hollows in wood warped by the job. His thoughts are racing, ideas bouncing and dancing, butchery is the oldest profession in the world, the future will be technological, electronic, and digital, there will be flying cars and intelligent robots, but butchers will still be around with their soiled aprons, their ties, and their filet mignons.

He leaps from one thought to the next, lost in contemplation of the long slot that houses his knife collection.

Hanging before him, obediently aligned, pieces of meat await preparation, fresh rubbery cuts that need to dry out so the muscles can slacken, so the tensed fibers can erase the memory of death, the memory of the slaughterhouse. Pim selects a fine-looking oxidized cut, tinged smoky red, takes a noisy whiff, lays it on the wood surface, removes the skin using a large malleable knife, tosses fat and nerves into a stainless-steel container. With the tip of his blade he sends white scraps flying. He assesses the hard bits, sets them aside to make ground beef, works a flank, switches to a small rigid boning knife, follows the curve of the bone, the crest, tackles a lamb with a chop of the meat cleaver at the last vertebrae, then removes the rib bones and extracts the lamb chops from the chest. Left hand placed flat beside the rib steak, the right one carves the thick meat, which falls in slices onto the block, it falls slow and limp, it sways before landing with a dry thump. Next up is the huge, well-worn slicer, the saw that cuts spare ribs, the steel that sharpens knife edges, the blade that scrapes and circles the bone, trims the meat, dives in and resurfaces like a seamstress with her needle, that weaves through and slips beneath the darkened outer layer—the butcher is in fact a dancer.

Two lamb carcasses wait at the end of the block, curled in the fetal position, back legs tied. Some people would be put off, they'd see themselves, recognize themselves, an association is made and then—an indelible image—it's their own legs trussed up on the workbench, ready to be carved. They avert their eyes but too late, they're even surprised not to be there, instead of the animal: that could be me on the butcher's block, its legs are my legs.

Better not to see the carcass, better not to enter the back room otherwise you're screwed.

The butcher is crying, it's been a while. Fatigue, perhaps. Round and inordinately salty tears appear in the corners of his eyelids, roll down, fall onto the meat like tiny bombs that explode upon contact with the animal flesh. Pim is crying over a rump steak. The red flesh darkens slightly, speckled with tiny spots, he's crying onto the meat, Pim is sobbing, he grabs the cut of beef, brings it to his mouth and licks the taste of blood and salt, now he places it against his puffy, burning eyes, the cold muscle provides relief and dries his pointless tears.

Yet again wild ideas pop into his head, his beef-addled brain: what if he were to slip naked inside a still-lukewarm animal, step into another being's skin, a day in the life, nestle inside its insides then sew the creature shut with a large needle and fishing line to hold in the warmth, to facilitate a heat exchange, immersion suit donned, Pim bivouacked inside a carcass, safe and sound.

Pim the man is now Pim the beast, he changes kingdoms, switches sides by way of this thermal connection of varying degrees of heat. It's not that he lows and grazes, it's not that he grows udders, it's that Pim is inhabiting an animal, they are indistinguishable, intermingled, more so than Pinocchio in the belly of the whale, and it's a fact, butchers spend more time with cold animals than with warm humans. The meat has transformed him into a sorcerer dancing across rib-eye steaks the way some dance across hot coals and atop a volcano, an epileptic seized with rapture and convulsions.

Pim locks himself inside the storage room, weaves around pieces of meat sleeping upside down, a kaleidoscope of colors, he makes his way between carcasses swaying like hanged men, half-steers, massive legs, a forest of fleshy stalactites attached to steel rods. The cold tenderizes the meat and seeps into Pim's bones. On the floor, pork meatballs soak in buckets, on the shelves, livers doze beside towering thick rib steaks.

Pim gets into position, ready to deliver an uppercut, to pummel the meat, legs bent, arms relaxed, he punches the carcasses barehanded, hits like a man possessed, his fist barely makes a dent in the dense, unmoving mass, it slips off exposed ribs, off the irregularities and depressions in the taut meat, heavy as ten punching bags, he roars, drunk with rage and ecstasy, hopping around his opponent in search of footholds but he can't get in a good blow, the meat's putting up a fight, his skin reddens, inflamed, scratched. He keeps punching, short of breath, his hands bleeding—hemorrhaging in both corners of the ring, Pim doesn't feel the pain, his fingers are anesthetized by the cold, he grabs a filet that he places on the wound to calm the burning and encourage healing, because meat taken straight from the animal is still full of life and because life is transmittable.

For example, a calf's liver slipped into Eddy Merckx's briefs in April 1973 during the Paris–Roubaix race. The bicycle seat's hard and rough surface rubs painfully against the skin of his buttocks, which are covered with saddle sores, bruises, and chafe marks. Eddy, ever stoic, doesn't complain, he keeps pedaling, but his face, pale and gaunt from the pain, black rings etched beneath his eyes, betrays the wounds. A butcher is located in the next town on the circuit: fists pound the roll-up door, two handsome livers are purchased, one for each cheek, the cyclist drops his pants during a pit stop, the medic attaches the meat with surgical tape, pants up and back on the saddle, Eddy resumes the race. Ass assuaged by the raw flesh, by the soft and cool touch of the meat, a second skin, tissues are regenerating and Eddy finds renewed hope, he's brought back to life, he pedals toward victory.

Meat is full of life and life is transmittable.

Pim, bloodied but soothed, unhooks a haunch of beef that he clutches to his chest like a friend discovered still alive on the battlefield once the cannon powder has cleared. They dance, him and the carcass, and this dance is a trance. Pim stops to fetch the battery-powered radio, tunes it to a classical station, and the waltz resumes. The radio is playing the overture of *The Magic Flute*, he and the meat are slowly spinning. Now the cut of beef on his shoulder is a wounded comrade he must carry to the infirmary. The meat is a trophy, an offering, a spoil of war, the firm flesh weighs heavy in his arms, soon it will be chopped into a million pieces but in this cold room it is still monumental, still sublime. Pim is surrounded by meat, submerged, he slumps onto the tiled floor and falls asleep for just a moment, a dense, black slumber, cheek pressed against a beef rump: he dreams and in his dream he is walking toward red, a sea and a desert, beneath a scarlet sky and across a fiery plain. Everything before him is monochromatic, blinding, up and down are indistinguishable, an endless block of red and his shadow sinking in. The color has fully invaded, Pim is walking, floating, in the red, a magnificent breach, weightless swan dives, every other color has disappeared and this one is so intense, so bright that it's intoxicating and electrifying.

Pim is roused by the biting cold and the fear of dying of a hypothermia as lethal as it would be stupid. He opens his eyes, gaze scattered, breathing frenetic, skin at saturation, the animals' bodies turned inside out like gloves.

Animals are lucky, they've been granted an interior life, and Pim wishes he too could see what's on the inside, that he could remove his own skin, gently peel it off to reach the mystery— the mystery of Pim—and what would his entrails tell us? The haruspex would come to read in them his muddled thoughts and rawest desires. Why settle for being an impermeable surface, Pim? Do you have a heart? a stomach? innards? On the scans, in the MRI, the images are hazy and opaque, the images are in black and white.

It's decided: Pim will donate his body to science so he can finally be chopped up and put on display. He's going to obtain an organ donor card, sign a release form, designate someone he trusts, leave everything to medicine. Yes, Pim, lost, and drunk on color, has made up his mind, a literal self-sacrifice because this is my body.

Butchers are superior to us because they're not afraid of blood, they're not terrorized by the meat hiding inside us and that we refuse to visualize.

Let's try for a second, close our eyes, make an effort, concentrate, let's imagine it, we're nothing but a heap of meat, a shapeless, blood-streaked mass behind the tidy arrangement that is our skin, our facial features, let's proceed with the tragic discovery of what lies beneath, the hidden face, the truth in other words, definitive and implacable, tails instead of heads. When I smile, when I cry, what's it like on the inside, on the other side of my mouth, my eyes, my cheekbones? Does my flesh warp like trembling earth pushed up by tectonic plates?

There's not another living soul in the cold room, there's only Pim, who's imagining himself as amorphous as his cuts of beef and who isn't afraid, there's only us who know that if our flesh was laid bare, we would suffer, we would weep, we would beg for mommy and someone call 911, because we're fine being heaps of meat but we don't want anyone to see.

Pim wants to learn everything about meat, beast and man, and goes online to order various resources, which he reads thanks to his recurring insomnia: dissertations about the evolution of the slaughterhouse, meat-based cookbooks, crime novels starring butcher-murderers, firsthand accounts of bison hunts, anthropological studies of cooking techniques, an illustrated encyclopedia of cattle farming, the sociology of butchery in the Charolais region, the history of the Wars of Religion—starving Parisians sustained themselves on bread made from human bones (the catacombs were exhumed and the skeletons coarsely ground into flour).

There's also the logbook kept by a Nenets reindeer herder on the Yamal Peninsula. Every two weeks, the Nenets slaughter a reindeer then consume its meat raw, seated in a circle around the animal, directly on the ground of the Siberian tundra. The children drink steaming blood from enameled cups and chew on bits of meat clinging to the animal's jaw, the parents cut up the hide to make coats, slippers, and shelters. Pim would love to join these forty thousand nomads scattered between the White Sea and the Yenisei River, Pim would love to wander this hostile land that extends all the way to the Arctic Circle, where meat is sold for five rubles a kilo, where pink-hued cuts of reindeer don't need a fridge to be preserved, the Siberian wind freezes them perfectly, a wind that screams low to the ground and lifts the snow in polar cyclones. Pim would love to wrap himself up in a reindeer hide the colors of the steppe.

Pim reads the same way he carves meat: diligently and doggedly. Pim is a simple, easygoing guy who is completely consumed, subsumed, by his activities, de-sinewing meat and reading—you are what you do.

Tonight he's reading a thick book about the history of cannibalism and imagining himself as chief of the Amazonian Tupinambá people, long hair gleaming like black diamonds. Pim is a wide-eyed wandering child who drowns himself in his readings.

He is a Tupinambá warrior who lives naked and free on the Brazilian coast, at the mouth of the Amazon River, turquoise feathers in his hair, arabesque patterns painted on his chest. Life is sweet and steady, picking cassava roots and sweet potatoes in the cool hours of dawn, carving rowboats for fishing, constructing terracotta bowls, weaving beautiful textiles.

Except eventually the white colonists make landfall, they're cruel, arrogant, and deadly, and the Tupinambá have no choice but to devour them: it's war and war means consuming your enemy's body, to consume them is to respect them. After the killing the bodies aren't left to rot, they're not tossed to wild beasts that would tear them apart without care and without ritual, they're eaten and this eating is revenge, in memory of offenses committed. Pim is the great predator, the Tupinambá jaguar who eats the body of his enemy while others eat the body of Christ. His adversary is game meat that he crudely prepares, it cooks for hours and becomes hard, charred. Then he dances around the purifying fire that burns up the insult and outrage, he expels the hostile souls, the white man is gone, devoured, the white man who will be grateful that the jaguar-warrior didn't leave him on the ground to become worm food.

Pim is a jaguar, a divine, magical creature, he also eats his dearly departed, he assimilates their virtues and their loving memory, he doesn't allow these cherished bodies to disappear, he grieves for them. For the Tupinambá the body is a sepulcher, the memory of a unifying bond, a life remembered; their meat simmers gently now it's inside of you, tender and spicy. The remains of the dead are cooked with grilled corn, the bones finely crushed and the powder mixed with mashed bananas. The tribe gathers around a fire, they sing, pray, meditate, and they eat, the feast of the dead.

The youngest Tupinambá disgustedly agree to this sacred duty imposed by their parents, sometimes they vomit a piece that is too mummified or the opposite, too fresh, and the elders give them a harsh look. Then revulsion gives way to the joy of a duty done, the joy of celebrating the deceased with dignity. They learn to gulp down their family and friends, and it's no easy task, even with seasonings.

Everything we swallow should make us better, make us stronger. Everything we swallow forms and transforms us, we are all the digested dead, we are all mixed, it's crowded inside. When you were alive, Father, I liked your face, yours was the face I watched, I spoke to. Now that you're dead, it's your meat I like, Father, yours is the meat that I devour and absorb, that's what links us from here on in.

Pim eventually falls asleep to these fantastical cannibalistic visions, he leaves the Amazon for New Guinea, now he's living with the Papuans, who cook wild pigs in earth ovens.

The forest is dense and dark green, a morning mist spreading above the treetops, the echo of voices carries far and Pim, barefoot, struggles to make his way down the narrow path that leads to the village. Today is the pig festival and preparations are underway for this rare and precious feast, families have gathered and contributed everything they own, garden harvests and animals.

Every family both owns a pig and nurtures it: the pampered creature, bred and fed, is a member of the community, but the day comes when it must go. As wild pigs get older they become obese and dangerous, at which point they must be slaughtered and often tears are shed when it's time to eat them. One last hug, pet them for a while, and a tender delousing.

A man releases an arrow that lands in the creature's side, it grunts at death, gushing blood, struggling to no avail, its hind leg attached to a stake. Pim averts his gaze but the others hurl abuse at him, they force him to look, to look the pig in the eyes, the eyes house the soul, the soul that will soon wither to nothing once the animal's eyelids shut for the final time. The Papuans form a circle around the dying creature, they're watching out for fluttering eyelids, for the evaporation of the soul.

Then the animal is carved up and the pieces shared, everyone takes a bite of another's pig—you never eat your own pig!—a savory slice of lung traded for some fatty ribs, the Papuans eat quickly, fervently, but never to excess. The meat was cooked in banana leaves, which gives it a strange sweet, lemony flavor, Pim can taste it on his lips like ChapStick. They eat, they sing and dance, his head is spinning, the cold of night falls like an ax, the carcass of the butchered animal is turning blue in the darkness, Pim is sinking, lulled by the laughter, by the voices of the Papuans hailing him in the distance, in soon-to-be imperceptible intonations.

Pim has dedicated his life to butchery and now people come from far away to buy his meat. But success hasn't affected his humility, it hasn't lessened his focus or altered his temperament, life slides past him without leaving a mark, not a single shadow, life flows by unimpeded, no accidents or notable events, an existence both incredibly flat, a calm empty sea, and raging. Meat is everything, his entire existence, though there are girls sometimes, temporal and sensory interludes, girls who throw themselves at the gentle butcher like a starving gaucho at a bison steak. They throw themselves at Pim's wiry body, his steady, inordinately large hands that caress them for hours and hours, it's indecent really. They're regular customers, the veterinarian at Rungis or a divorcée he met online. He never discusses meat with these women, he doesn't want to bore anyone, he listens as they tell him about their day, he kisses them, cooks them rack of veal and ham hock at their place, then they sleep together, in silence. He refuses to choose one and give up the others, he doesn't want to settle down with a single woman, one for example who might like sirloin steak but not shoulder, Bresse chicken but not beef cheeks. A single woman would limit the pleasure and the possibilities. But the truth is that if Pim wanted to marry one of his lovers he would be taking the risk of being left because women always leave butchers; butchers are divorced or single. Too much work on the one hand, too much solitude on the other, their partners lose patience, they take off, weary of being underappreciated. Pim wouldn't know how to keep any of them. The evenings he spends with one lover then another, slow-roasted or pan-fried, are a shared, consensual pleasure, and that's enough; they don't demand anything, they don't expect more than what's offered, these are modern women without delusions of grandeur and who like to eat.

They get used to Pim's strange lover ways, to the fact that he seems to take more pleasure from cooking a rabbit in mustard sauce—cooking for them, mind you—than from fooling around. And the fact that he can't envisage the slightest sexual activity before having grilled a steak or roasted a guinea hen.

Some of the women try to reverse the evening's sequence, leaping at him as soon as he arrives, tearing the pretty package wrapped in gingham paper with a matching satin ribbon out of his hands, then authoritatively leading him to the bed, ripping his clothes off without interruption of the preliminary kissing—a perilous gymnastic feat—and finally hopping on top of the butcher.

But it stops there; the butcher's gone soft.

Then, seated before a flank steak cooked with shallots, his drive comes back, his taste for flesh returns.

One night Pim consoles a woman who bursts into tears when the butcher offers her the umpteenth roast presented like a trophy. A woman, a lover, who can no longer bear the sight of meat, a woman oppressed by meat, who has developed hang-ups because of meat, meat that is nothing more than a vain display of flesh in robust health, an explosion of life and if it spoils toss it to the stray dogs. *Meanwhile I feel so old. I feel myself becoming inedible.*

What cruelty, what injustice, this inequality between meats, this way we have of thinking about death. Falling in love with a butcher is not a risk-free endeavor, not when he's shoving that beautiful arrogant meat in your face.

She's aging, imperceptibly at first, every day brings tiny internal landslides, minuscule earthquakes that just barely shake the body from the inside, a slight quivering of the skin, a wrinkle, a membrane that slackens, and one day a clear vision of the deterioration that's begun, concern and then dread that hardens her good humor and desire. Now she's on the lookout for visible changes in her body, the little belly that bloats then droops and puckers, the hunched posture, she no longer sees herself as very appetizing when she looks in the mirror though Pim would love to gobble her up, Pim who feels as robust as a rib-eye, though he wishes he could reassure her, *you're beautiful you're vibrant and delicious*, but the woman isn't fooled by Pim's sweetness, by a lover's sincerity, the woman know what it means to love, it means you tenderize reality. *In any case the best meat is always aged*—this makes her laugh through her tears.

Pim is still honing his craft in the aim of becoming the world's best butcher. The days are long, hypnotic and exhausting, and the few hours he spends resting in his studio above the shop are filled with thoughts of butchery. It's all he thinks about, the entirety of his mental space now dedicated to this obsession.

What else could I do with meat, to elevate the art of butchery? As he tries to fall asleep, laying on a single mattress on the floor, Pim counts wild possibilities the way other people do sheep.

Idea no. 1: receive a transfusion of pure cow's blood and/ or receive a liver transplant from a pig. Pim's willing to give it a try. He looked online to see if a Californian clinic offered it, if they were looking for volunteers. He found far worse: a man offering his body as a banquet. Kill me, carve me, cook me, and eat my meat while toasting to my good health (*I pair nicely with a Châteauneuf-du-Pape '98*).

And why not get a beautiful snout transplant, gleaming like enamel? Or have his feet amputated and replaced by hog hooves that would miraculously slide into a pair of calf-hair heels.

Idea no. 2: put on a show with sheep cows pigs chickens. Hogs balancing on a wire, Holstein acrobats, tamed guinea fowl, a lamb with a red nose, and a fire-breathing calf. Pim as the ringmaster, houndstooth suit and a white apron, a pig on a spit at intermission.

Idea no. 3: find a job with a traveling circus. Pim could be the butcher-juggler, knife juggler, or cleaver swallower. Anything goes, a boning paring chopping skinning carving breaking filleting knife and then, the pièce de résistance, a cleaver that concludes its careening flight in a rack of ribs balanced on the head of a young maiden tied to a wooden board.

Idea no. 4: reopen the city's slaughterhouses, go back to the era of man and beast in close quarters, hand in hoof, when every butcher had an abattoir adjoining his stand, when blood flowed through the cobblestone, muddy streets, curdling beneath pedestrians' feet, when sewers were primitive, when garbage would pile up outside butcher stalls, when the smell of decomposing meat deliciously oxidized the air (and damn Napoleon who in 1810 decided to clean up the city and build five slaughterhouses on the outskirts of Paris). Pick up the farmer's ax, deal the fatal blow beneath the tall oaks, beside the babbling brook, and watch the blood as it contaminates the communal water supply.

Thing is, Pim wants to go down in the history of butchery, his name written in ink, and for that he needs to do something big, do the craft justice, reach his full potential, achieve his mission, his sublime task. But sometimes Pim senses the bitter taste of incompletion in his mouth. *There's still more to be done for meat, something grander.*

A growing excitement, a swelling hope—the hope of seeing it through, of reaching a finish line so distant it looks like a dot, bright as a star.

Every night he thinks about his mission hard enough to set his temporal veins throbbing, and finally one morning he knows. It's like everyone: you search, you devise, then, after long marination, your intentions surge forth, clear and indubitable.

Pim has a plan.

III

Pim's going to liberate butchery, wage the ultimate battle, confront the meat.

Pim's going to bring the art of butchery to its zenith, he knows how, he knows what he's been missing, it's time for the grand finale, it's time for the big finish and the moment of truth.

Pim remembers his internship at the cattle farm in Pays de Caux, he remembers Culotte the cow, the rugged animals in the barn. He's never gone back, hasn't kept in touch.

He remembers the little road that leads from the Bréauté-Beuzeville train station to the farm.

Pim gets into his van around 10:00 p.m., takes the Saint-Cloud exit to highway A13, drives, passes the Tancarville Bridge, drives, Saint-Eustache-la-Forêt, Beuzeville-la-Grenier, drives, reaches his destination a little after midnight, and parks just off the road. He recognizes his surroundings, nothing appears to have changed, the barn is still there, the cattle farmer undoubtedly deceased and Culotte cut up into steaks a long time ago.

Pim climbs over the fence, creeping like a cat in the dark, not a single lit-up window, not a single barking dog, the turkeys are sleeping like logs, a dull silence barely broken by the rustling of leaves, Pim isn't afraid at all, it doesn't even occur to him that the farmer might come out, rifle in hand, alerted by the unusual movements, everything is asleep.

He slinks, hunched over, all the way to the barn, the door squeaks slightly, he slips inside and makes his way in the dark just as he would have in broad daylight, his body having retained the building's exact layout and the placement of its occupants. As he passes, a few cows tap the ground with nervous hooves. He strides over to Culotte's former stall, near the back. There's a cow sprawled out asleep, breathing loudly, he kneels down cautiously and whispers in her ear, his mouth grazing the big, silky auricle: *I owe you cows a lot and tonight I've decided to set you free.* He stands up and now he loudly stirs up the indifferent crowd: *I'm going to set all of you free. But listen up, you won't be leaving together, it's every cow for herself . . . and the hunt is on!*

The cow—maybe Culotte's daughter, Culotte II or Culotte Jr.—still motionless, has opened one eye, sleepy gaze fixed on the ground. Pim stretches out beside her in the straw. Nestled against the animal's flank, he waits, idles away the remaining time, reaches into his pocket for a flask of brandy, an Armagnac that'll strip your mucous membranes clean.

He removes the cap, proffers the flask before the animal's nostrils like a vial of smelling salts under a courtesan's nose, the cow's snout quivers slightly, Pim takes a swig, clicks his tongue, snorts, feels the oaky liquid free-fall into his intestines like a ball of fire. He empties the bottle with small toxic gulps, still leaning against the cow, a block of welcoming curves. The heat of the animal and the heat of the alcohol mix and intensify inside Pim's body as he sinks into a brutal, inebriated torpor. The alcohol's been drunk to the dregs, his stomach is burning, his mouth is dry and acrid, his eyes tinged with yellow, he's rabid.

When the large wall clock in the barn shows 4:00 a.m., Pim leaps up, a stab of pain at his temples, he runs to the opposite end of the barn, opens the doors then wakes up the cows one by one, pushes them toward the exit with a series of smacks on their hindquarters. They resist, perturbed by these unfamiliar maneuvers. On the farm side nothing moves. Pim forces the cows down the path to the road. Miraculously they fall into single file and begin to advance, guided by the butcher's voice, he opens the gate, lets them out and leaves them there, packed together in the middle of the road, disconcerted.

A frozen horde of cows who don't understand that they're free, that they're being ordered to be free, to return to their natural and wild state. A compact throng of animals beneath the stars futilely rubbing their muzzles against the asphalt in search of grass to graze, who expect nothing but the pressure of the breeder's hand on their teats. But there's no grazing or milking, just a long ribbon fading into the horizon, black and hard beneath their hooves, and the sidereal void of night. The cows don't move, glued together, they've lost their bearings, they're waiting, they're waiting for reasonable instructions, they're waiting for routine to resume, but now Pim is shouting and blindly hitting them with a stick: *Go on, you're free, come on, go, go!* He gesticulates for several minutes, out of breath, before a first cow emerges from her stupor and begins to move. Leaving the herd, she advances slowly in the direction of the town. Pim watches her gain distance, she's walking on the right side of the road, her pace steady, she doesn't turn around and soon disappears around a bend; her large round hindquarters reappear one final time, awkwardly undulating. Copying her, a second cow begins to walk then suddenly gallops, like she's just received an electric shock, after the first, hoping perhaps to catch up with her at the bend. Gradually, at Pim's steady encouragement, the animals get underway one behind the other. Now they're taking up the middle of the road, down the white line, and heading toward the town, the unlikely direction chosen by the first among them, the bravest or the most oblivious. A hundred cows disappear over the horizon in a long procession, their gait is heavy and hesitant, but not one turns around or slows down.

He watches them disappear, impassive. At this early hour the road is deserted, no cars to hinder their flight, their exile, their rout, their journey, how else to put it? But what becomes of liberated cows, of animals created for domestication? Set free in the middle of Normandy, abandoned to their own devices, they certainly won't survive, they won't adapt to the ferocity of the laws of nature. Cows aren't made for this, they never learned to find food on their own, to lick their injuries to encourage healing, to treat their mastitis, udders red and swollen, to give birth without the assistance of a veterinarian, his or her expert gloved hand digging deep for the hoof of a poorly positioned calf, they never learned how to defend themselves from wild weasels, hungry wolves, killer hens, cunning foxes, stray dogs, and Pim the butcher. They'll get themselves devoured by the first beast of the field they encounter, unless they devour each other that is. Then the vultures will show up, drawn all the way from the Grand Canyon by this new carnivorous treat, and tear the bovines apart in the wooded countryside. From now on, by the grace of Pim, Normandy is a jungle, a savanna, a savage and merciless forest, without god or law except survival of the fittest. Pim declares a state of nature, fences down, man and beast stranded in the wild. Pim is now the first man, surrounded by pastures, trees, and thickets, surrounded by animals that number in the millions.

Pim wants to return to a simpler time, one on one, when man truly understood the animal he was preparing to eat. And this because he had hunted the animal, butchered and cooked it, sometimes he had had time to observe it, to admire it for hours, to lie in wait before throwing his harpoon. On occasion the man would even meet the animal's eye in the instant the fatal arrow was released. Yes, this primitive era is what Pim aspires to today.

He is the butcher who stepped off of Noah's ark, the butcher who came after the Flood and set foot on dry land with his procession of saved animals. Pim is the original butcher, he's the one who drives the goat into the wilderness.

God said to Noah: *You are to bring into the ark two of all living creatures, male and female, to keep them alive with you. Two of every kind of bird, of every kind of animal and of every kind of creature that moves along the ground will come to you to be kept alive.*

Then came the flood, the end of the rains, and Noah waited for the earth to dry before leaving the ark, followed by his wife, his children, and Pim, a stowaway hiding in the hold.

Then God said to Noah: *Everything that lives and moves will be food for you. Just as I gave you the green plants, I now give you everything.*

And thus humankind became carnivorous and Pim its first butcher, because now one was needed. He was the first man to kill an animal, and it took great courage to catch the beast, to immobilize it, slit its throat, and remove its skin, to be the first man to kill the wild creature running beneath the bright sun, basking in the tall grass that grew after the flood, bleating to the sky and inhaling the rain-saturated air. Pim wants to be the first carnivore. There won't be any going back. Pim, your act will be an act for the ages: the eating of animals.

This is what Pim is hoping for today, on this country road as the cows scatter into the wild, the barn deserted. Here's his plan: release the cows then chase them. Toreador- or cowboy-style. The countryside is an arena, the duel matched. The countryside is a vast plain in the Wild West, pounded by sun and dust. Pim gets in the saddle and sets out on this Norman hunt like he's hunting bison, riding through the arid canyons of Utah, lasso tight in his left hand, reins coiled in his right, rifle on his back, Pim thinks he's Buffalo Bill and his Stetson is black with sweat and grime.

Pim wants the wild cow in his crosshairs, wants to bring it down with a single bullet lodged behind its ear, then he'll dismember the beast, flay it, butcher it, and remove the skin, which will be folded and stuffed in the old leather bag hanging from his saddle. Then: cut off its head, as a trophy, and bring it back carefully balanced on his horse's neck. Pim will be the butcher-hunter. No more cattle farms, no more slaughterhouses, simply every butcher armed with a rifle, who will sell the animal killed with their own hands to a customer who will be told, as a bonus, the story of the hunt: *The sun was setting, it was getting hard to see, it had been hours since I started tracking a pretty little Charolais with a flashy coat, copper-colored in the last rays of sunlight, and then she moved behind a thicket, I fired, stroke of luck, I got her on the first shot, and now look, a nice little flank steak, what else can I get for you?*

Pim imagines his stand in town, the open-air chopping block on which he'll carve before his customers' eyes the animal fresh from the slaughter and giving off the smell of lichen and musk.

Pim wants to restore butchery as it was, fair and square, a face-off between man and cow, man and hog, bare knuckles in the mud if needed. Pim will brave the possibility of being injured or even devoured by a pig in his quest to reinstate the grand exchange of the living. To be eaten by a cow rather than by worms six feet under. To be a Sioux hunter who leaves corpses out in the open for the wild animals, to inhabit a new world in which herds once fenced in by man are now free, that's to say game like all the rest, a pig equals a puma, a cow equals a caribou. A world in which there are no more grazing pastures, no more barbed wire, pens, or fields, but land as far as the eye can see, thick and hostile vegetation that you have to cut through with a machete or chainsaw. Normandy is beautiful and epic, overrun by brambles, blanketed by forests of oaks and apple trees, the grass is tall, the ground soft and damp.

Let's just say that Pim wants to start the butcher revolution, the great backward leap, he wants to rediscover the reason of animals and the taste of meat.

Feet still planted in the middle of the silent road, Pim is imagining virgin expanses and savage corridas, the sun is up now, the cows have disappeared from view, involuntary runaways. A shiver runs through him, the morning dew cools the air and pulls him from his reveries. Coolness but there's also a warm breath on his neck, a dark, unmoving, and familiar mass behind him. Someone's there. It's Culotte Jr. Perfectly still, as though her four hooves are nailed to the ground. She's the last one, she didn't obey the butcher's orders. Pim turns to face this creature solemnly staring at him. Her sharp pupils stand out in the opaque dawn light, her long eyelashes dangling; suddenly they begin to flutter frenetically, like a nervous tic, the cow blinks her eyes in rapid succession, as though something is irritating or blinding her. The animal is marble but her gaze has been taken hostage by some great agitating force, her eyelids now moving uncontrollably—Morse code?

What are you doing here? Go on, scram. Go join your friends, don't worry, we'll meet again, I'll make you into the nicest steak there ever was, I'll put you on display on a gold platter, now go, goddammit!

The cow is a pillar of salt, and her twitchy troubling gaze a beacon of distress, a stroboscopic pulse.

Stop blinking, you're driving me crazy!

Before the uninterrupted heat of the animal's gaze he starts to feel dizzy, a queasy curtain descends in his brain, his pulse is beating too fast at his temples, his heart is thumping like a subwoofer and soon it will tear apart his rib cage. Pim screams with rage: *You're a coward cow, you're backing down, you won't put up a fight, you'd rather be a slave!*—this unfair cow who refuses freedom, and Pim who's imagining the animal's cloudy eye at the end of his barrel. *Since there's no getting through to you . . .* Pim goes to his van to get his semiautomatic Browning rifle—purchased online for 1,700 euros—and fires a first shot in the air: the cow starts and totters on her front hooves, he takes aim while letting out a battle cry that echoes across the empty countryside; finally, she's moving, she's running, the hunt is on.

The crazed creature gets herself tangled in barbed wire, Pim frees her and opens the pasture gate, she gallops toward the horizon, flees across the fields like a clumsy gazelle.

Pim gives her a thirty-second head start and then, taking the same route, goes after her. His long legs carry him easily, he runs almost without effort, mechanically, oxygen to spare, long and steady strides, Pim feels light and fleet, the landscape unfolding in forward tracking, the soft ground cushions his feet, he glimpses her in the distance, a motionless dot at first, he gets closer and the dot grows and takes shape, there she is grazing serenely in the shade of a thicket, the oblivious creature is right in front of him, she didn't even notice him, too busy bolting down meadow grass.

The butcher drops and lies down on the lush ground, he melts into the soil, flat as a beet field, rifle extended along his arm, body frozen and tense as a bow, one dilated pupil focusing, finger on the trigger, he takes aim at the cow, holds his breath, and shoots, a single bullet, a muffled explosion, bang, that penetrates midchest, glides horizontally into the animal's body without encountering any resistance or being halted by an organ, it slides through the meat like a bobsled careening across ice at the speed of sound and comes out the other end of the cow, just above the tail, the projectile's trajectory perfectly rectilinear, an unbelievable shot—if you placed your eye against the point of entry, you'd see into the cow as if through a telescope.

She stiffens then collapses with all her weight onto her left flank, hooves limp. Pim waits a few seconds, then gently crawls to the animal that's no longer breathing, lifeless.

The butcher kneels, pushes up his jacket sleeves, grabs hold of the cow's head by one horn, and without hesitation draws his knife from a leather sheath attached to his belt, slits the beast's throat with one confident movement, a single stroke. Pim is talented; the blood gushes. He stands up and now he's going to butcher the animal.

He didn't bring his knife kit, too cumbersome, and has to conduct the entire operation with a single blade, a skinning knife with a rosewood handle. Its long edge can be used for deboning, while its forward-curving blade facilitates the cutting of hides.

Pim runs the blade around the cow's neck to remove the head—a muscle memory from the slaughterhouse— the thick, elastic skin resists, the blade struggles against cartilage, he forces it, insistent, hands sore, muscles on fire, shirt drenched, powers through, then, for two hours as the sun rises, he skins and removes the animal's hide. It separates easily from the flesh, Pim rolls the massive skin up like a carpet, a bloody wall hanging. The heat radiating from the beast's entrails protects him from the wet cold of the Normandy dawn. Once he's flayed the entire cow with the tip of his knife, he can finally open her up, one deep, straight cut, and plunge into her insides the better to extract them: his long arms buried, his febrile hands rummaging, a gentle, lukewarm bath. He blindly gropes the intestines, the heart, the rumen—Pim covered in blood, soiled like a child, blood and sweat blended into a greasy liquid and the reddening grass around him forming a tragic halo. He tosses away the viscera, then cuts off the udders, struggles to saw off the hooves, severs the tail, and then, the sun very high, very yellow, he begins to carve.

The butcher methodically separates each piece, in anatomical order, faithfully following the curve of the meat, the path of the nerves and the ligaments. Flank, mock tender, shoulder, tri-tip, chuck eye, every element is removed then arranged outside of the animal, on the ground, according to its original geography, every piece in its place. Pim, meticulous, puts the cow and all its parts back together, assembles the puzzle of its organs in the open air, a cow that's been skinned, cut open, and laid flat, a cow that in the butcher's hands goes from 3D to 2D. Seen from the sky, the meat looks like a map, an anatomical chart in flesh and bones, everything's there, nothing's missing, a perfect tableau, irreproachable execution, the dissection complete. A butchered carcass and next to it a reconstructed cow, a cow in the raw, all the butcher's cuts.

Pim has just killed his first beast. He topples backward, arms outstretched, sprawls out on the cool ground, exultant, eyes glistening. The countryside is deserted and mute, the air iridescent, the damp earth has absorbed and diluted the animal's blood, the surroundings appear immense and flat, a deep, luminous backdrop.

Pim, exhausted and proud, feels his muscles relaxing, adrenaline dissipating and slowing its mad race through his veins, his hands growing cold and blood drying on his fingers while a carnivorous love pours out of him, an insensate gratitude for the animals he loves and eats, that he loves and kills. Blinding sun, eyes shut, shadows dancing and blinking, his head is heavy, it drops slightly, he's dreaming of the first butcher, the butcher he would have liked to be, of the first sacrificer armed with the first blade, of the first domesticated beast, the first enclosure, the first flames beneath scarlet flesh, the first meal, he dreams of their shared fate, of the intermingled lives of cow and man, he dreams of meat, the meat invented by humanity in the wake of the flood.

AUTHOR'S ACKNOWLEDGMENTS

I owe many thanks to Patrice David, a butcher in Vanves.

As well as to all the authors whose works inspired and accompanied me during the writing of this book: Stéphane Breton, Jean-Luc Daub, Vinciane Despret, Élisabeth de Fontenay, Marcela Iacub, Dominique Lestel, Jocelyne Porcher, Jean Réal, Alina Reyes, Jonathan Safran Foer, Isabelle Sorente.

JOY SORMAN is a novelist and documentarian who lives and works in Paris. She has written fourteen books, including *Boy, boys, boys*, which was awarded the 2005 Prix de Flore, *La peau de l'ours*, *À la folie*, and *Sciences de la vie*, which was published by Restless Books in 2021 as *Life Sciences*. *Tenderloin*, for which she received the 2013 François Mauriac prize from l'Académie française, is Sorman's second novel to be translated into English.

LARA VERGNAUD is a translator of prose, creative nonfiction, and scholarly works from the French. She is the recipient of the French-American Foundation Translation Prize and the French Voices Grand Prize, and has been nominated for the National Translation Award. She lives in southern France.